Painted Skull Ranch

A Fernando Lopez Santa Fe Mystery

Also by James C. Wilson from Sunstone Press:

Hiking New Mexico's Chaco Canyon: The Trails, The Ruins, The History
Santa Fe, City of Refuge: An Improbable Memoir of the Counterculture

The Fernando Lopez Santa Fe Mystery Series:

Peyote Wolf
Smokescreen
Ghost Canyon
The Dead Go Fast
Painted Skull Ranch
Devil on Canyon Road

PAINTED SKULL RANCH

A FERNANDO LOPEZ SANTA FE MYSTERY

JAMES C. WILSON

SUNSTONE
PRESS

SANTA FE

Sunstone books may be purchased for educational, business, or sales promotional use.
For information please write: Special Markets Department, Sunstone Press,
P.O. Box 2321, Santa Fe, New Mexico 87504-2321.

Book and cover design › R. Ahl
Printed on acid-free paper

eBook 978-1-61139-698-8

Library of Congress Cataloging-in-Publication Data

Names: Wilson, James C., 1948- author. | Wilson, James C., 1948- Fernando
Lopez Santa Fe mystery.

Title: Painted Skull Ranch : a Fernando Lopez Santa Fe mystery / James C.
Wilson.
Description: Santa Fe : Sunstone Press, [2022] | Series: A Fernando Lopez Santa
Fe mystery

Summary: "When Santa Fe musician Danny Ortiz is murdered, Private
Investigator Fernando Lopez is hired by Ortiz's wife to find the killer. His
investigation takes Lopez to mysterious Painted Skull Ranch in Taos, a 200-year-
old haunted ranch where Lopez uncovers a viper's nest of greed, treachery, and
murder"-- Provided by publisher.

Identifiers: LCCN 2022047346 | ISBN 9781632934598 (paperback) | ISBN
9781611396898 (epub)

Subjects: LCSH: Lopez, Fernando (Fictitious character) | Murder--Investigation--
Fiction. | Country musicians--New Mexico--Fiction. | Ranches--New Mexico--
Taos--Fiction. | LCGFT: Detective and mystery fiction.

Classification: LCC PS3623.I58485 P35 2022 | DDC 813.6--dc23/eng/20221025
LC record available at https://lccn.loc.gov/2022047346

WWW.SUNSTONEPRESS.COM
SUNSTONE PRESS / POST OFFICE BOX 2321 / SANTA FE, NM 87504-2321 /USA
(505) 988-4418

Preface and Dedication

I grew up among the empty spaces of rural Nebraska in the 1950s. At bedtime, in the immense solitude of a Nebraska night, I would hunker down under my blankets and listen to music on my transistor radio in the darkness. Back then it was mostly the music of Buddy Holly coming all the way from Lubbock, Texas, that offered me a lifeline to the larger world.

As I got older and moved to the Southwest, I discovered a rich culture of singer/songwriters from Austin and Nashville whose songs and lyrics got me through some rough years. Still do, from time to time.

So, with gratitude, this book is dedicated to the memory of Buddy Holly, John Prine, Waylon Jennings, Johnny Cash, and old Jerry Jeff Walker, who drank a bit; and to the transcendent Emmylou Harris, the inimitable Willy Nelson, and the one and only Panama Red, Peter Rowan, whose "Free Mexican Air Force" will be flying tonight.

1

Danny Ortiz finished his second set just after ten p.m. He ended by singing the Willie Nelson version of "Always on my Mind," usually a crowd pleaser. Tonight, though, the few people left at the Coyote Bar and Grill seemed uninterested. So he concluded with his standard farewell, Bob Dylan's "Forever Young," which brought smiles to a few faces in the somber crowd and elicited muted applause. Afterwards he gathered together his picks and bridges and placed his Gibson in its carrying case and then went to the bar to pick up his check. Andy, the bartender, wandered over to meet him. As mindless as ever.

"Can I get you a drink? On the house?" Andy asked.

Danny shook his head. "No, I better get home. My wife's eight months pregnant and doesn't like it when I stay out late."

"Suit yourself."

"Do you have my check?" Danny asked.

"Yeah, it's in the office."

Andy went in back to get the check while he looked at his reflection in the mirror behind the bar. Danny didn't like the tired, haggard little man he saw looking back at him, with bags under his eyes and dark hair already streaked with gray. He was getting too old for this kind of work. He needed a regular gig he could count on at a more upscale venue.

Andy reappeared and handed him a check made out to Danny Ortiz for three hundred dollars.

"Does the boss want me next weekend?"

"Not sure. Ask him on Monday. The tourist season hasn't really started yet, so I don't know..."

He saluted, jealous of Andy's youth and good looks. Tall and well-toned with a shock of blond hair falling over his forehead, Andy looked like a Beach Boy, a real lady killer.

Danny deposited the check in his shirt pocket and grabbed his guitar case and headed for the door. On San Francisco Street a few people still loitered downtown, some sitting on benches in the Plaza. Out front of Starbucks a street musician played a violin for tips, a young woman named Greta who he'd hung around with some before his marriage. He reached in his pocket and pulled out a five-dollar bill, which he dropped in her violin case. Got to share the wealth. Sexy Greta winked at him as he walked by. He still remembered their good times, the nights he'd spent in her apartment. Hot in the sack, Greta was. Why did they ever break up? He couldn't remember. Too much alike, he supposed.

Danny congratulated himself. At least he didn't have to play on the street for tips. Not yet anyway. He kept thinking about what might have been had Dallas Longstreet not bailed on him. An A-lister from Austin famous for his Texas-inspired country rock, Dallas had been Danny's meal ticket for the past few years. Dallas had been generous to him, no doubt about it. He still had a check from Dallas in his wallet that he hadn't yet cashed. Dallas came to Santa Fe every year to perform at the Lensic Theater and other high profile venues in northern New Mexico. For the past ten years Danny had opened for Dallas at every show, as regular as the seasons. Danny needed the gigs more than ever this year now that his wife was pregnant and the baby due next month. Not planned, of course.

Sure, he knew Dallas had a drug problem, but it had never prevented him from putting on a good show. So he was surprised when Dallas showed up in Santa Fe and canceled his spring concert at the Lensic. Instead, Dallas had been hanging out in Taos with a friend named Travis Walker who was a well-known drug dealer and grifter from L.A. Travis had rented an old hacienda he named Painted Skull Ranch off Highway 64 east of Taos. The rustic guest ranch, as Travis called it, had become a gathering place for dopers, misfits, and lost souls looking for drugs and redemption. That was the last thing Dallas needed. Which is why Danny had tried— and failed—to talk Dallas into leaving the ranch and getting back on the circuit.

Walking by the La Fonda Hotel Danny decided to give it one more shot. Tomorrow morning he would drive up to Taos and again try to persuade Dallas to leave. That would be risky, because on his last visit a couple of tough guys working for Travis had kicked him off the premises and warned him not to return. The control Travis seemed to exert over Dallas worried him. So did the macabre furnishings with *memento mori* everywhere on the grounds and the creepy human skull with painted red eyes on top of a totem pole at the entrance to the ranch. The place and the people there looked like some sort of death cult to him. He didn't care what it was; he just wanted to get Dallas out of there so the two of them could work again. He desperately needed the income, even if Dallas didn't.

Danny crossed the street to the Cathedral and entered the park, his usual route when walking home to the rented duplex on Otero Street he shared with Oralia, his wife. Darkness enveloped him as he walked further into the park amid the shadows. Only a sprinkling of lights on Palace Avenue guided him. Up ahead near the Drury Hotel he heard voices, angry male voices. They seemed to be having a heated discussion. He paused, unsure of what to do. He didn't want to get mixed up in a heated argument that could turn violent. That was always a possibility these days when everyone seemed on edge and short-tempered. Should he circle back around to Palace or keep going? He decided to keep going, not wanting to waste time. He was exhausted from the long day and just wanted to crash.

Now Danny heard angry words and shouting. In the darkness he saw two men materialize out of the darkness. When they noticed him, the two men started wrestling with each other. He didn't recognize either of them. The bigger of the two slapped the other man in the face and then shoved him backwards. Surprised, the man fell and landed on his back. Then the big man pounced and the two of them rolled around on the wet grass wrestling. Moments later the smaller one appeared seriously hurt. He lay still in the grass moaning while the big guy jumped up and started kicking him—or pretended to kick him. What was that all about? The one on the ground cursed at his attacker and shouted out insults.

"Hey—cool it, don't hurt the guy!" Danny yelled, his instincts taking over. He set down his guitar case and hurried over to where the fallen man lay. The man wore a dark jacket and seemed to be unconscious.

The other man disappeared into the darkness.

Danny grabbed the fallen man's shoulders and shook him. "Are you okay? Can you hear me?"

The man mumbled something he couldn't understand.

"Do you want me to call for help?"

No response.

"Listen, do you want me to call nine-one-one?" he asked, again shaking the man by the shoulders. "Oh hell."

Danny stood up and reached for the cellphone in his back pocket. Suddenly he felt the air currents shift behind him. He thought he heard movement in the grass. He turned around just in time to see a fist coming toward him. It smashed into his face, sending him reeling backwards onto the ground. He felt his nose spurting blood and the sticky liquid flowing down his neck. His first thought was to get up and fight but he fell over when he attempted to get to his knees. He rolled around in the wet grass, too dazed to rise.

When his assailant tried to kick him he managed to grab a foot and twist it. Cursing, the man sprawled backwards and flailed about in the grass.

Danny tried to shout, to tell the man to leave him alone, but no sound came out of his mouth.

He struggled to his feet, looking around for his guitar case. He just wanted to get away. Fuck both of them. They could kill each other for all he cared.

Before he could take a step his assailant blocked his way. He thought he recognized the man. Where had he seen him?

Danny raised his hands as the blow came, striking him hard on the side of the face. He spun around and plunged face down into the wet grass. He felt the night dew on his face and tasted it on his tongue.

Then one of them jumped on his back, knocking the wind out of him. He couldn't breath. The man's hands wrapped around his neck and squeezed, choking off his air.

Letting go, he slipped into blackness.

2

Former detective Fernando Lopez spent the morning drinking coffee and reading the *Independent* on his back patio. He was glad to be back home in Santa Fe after an unpleasant two days in Denver chasing a Santa Fe businessman who it turned out had a second family tucked away in a cozy Denver suburb. The hardest part had been breaking the news to his Santa Fe wife, even though she'd begun to expect as much given her husband's long absences and lack of amorous attention, so to speak. After drying her tears, the wife had called her lawyer and started proceedings to divorce the sonofabitch. The cheating husband agreed to the divorce and an amicable division of their assets and headed back to Denver. Case closed.

What Fernando didn't understand about the situation was how any man—or woman for that matter—would have the time or energy to fool around with a second family. Didn't they have enough problems with the first? Some people never seemed to learn that time and energy were finite just like everything else in life, including life itself. Go figure.

Done brooding, he tossed the *Independent* in the trash where it belonged and headed out to his Jeep Cherokee, a gift from his wife Estelle when he retired from the Santa Fe Police Department last year. He drove down Acequia Madre to the Paseo and around to Canyon Road. His office was located a few blocks up Canyon Road in a remodeled garage owned by Ruby Montez that sat back behind her art gallery. An old friend from the doomed anti-gentrification wars of the nineties, Ruby had let him use the garage rent-free. She'd even allowed him to remodel the small structure into something resembling an office, with wood paneling on the walls and new carpet on the concrete floor. With a desk, bookshelves, and two sitting chairs, what else did he need?

Fernando parked in the gravel lot between Ruby's gallery and Essentia, the sex shop next door that sold sex toys and unguents for people who believed sex, like camping, required an assortment of gear.

Stepping out of the Cherokee he again had to stop and admire the hand-painted wooden sign at the rear of the parking lot: 'Fernando Lopez, Private Investigator' with an image of an elongated eye below the print. He walked over and opened the door, turning his sign from closed to open. Inside the office still smelled of new wood and carpet. He raised the side window to let in some fresh air and then sat down at his desk to admire his latest purchase, a mini refrigerator where he stored bottles of water and Modelo, his favorite beer.

He was about to boot up his laptop when he heard the crunch of footsteps approaching in the gravel parking lot.

A shadow appeared outside the door, another woman. Most of his customers so far had been women. That said something, but just what he wasn't sure. The woman opened the door slowly, tentatively. "Hello? Is anyone here?"

"Come in. Please."

The door opened wide, revealing a woman with a round moon face framed by long black hair. Obviously pregnant, she held both hands on her belly as though already cradling the unborn child. She wore a simple cotton smock with an elastic waist. She stopped when she saw him sitting at the desk. "Mr. Lopez?"

"Yes." He hurried across the room to help her to a chair. She looked vaguely familiar, but so did everyone else in Santa Fe if you'd lived here as long as he had. "Sorry I don't have anything more comfortable."

She nodded. "I'm fine. Really."

"How can I help you?"

"Well..." She paused for a long moment getting comfortable in the chair. "I'm Oralia Ortiz. My husband Danny was murdered Saturday night in Cathedral Park. You might have read about it in yesterday's newspaper?"

"Of course," Fernando said. "I'm so sorry. I heard him play many times. I loved his music."

She stared at him, tears forming in the corners of her eyes.

"The police think it was a random encounter, right?" Fernando asked. "That he just came across a couple of hoodlums in the dark and they robbed him?"

She shook her head, the tears now rolling down her cheeks. "That's what the police say, but I think they're wrong. It's true that money was taken from Danny's wallet, but I don't think it was an accident or a robbery because they didn't take his guitar, a Gibson Les Paul worth a small fortune. No, I think they planned to kill him. They knew Danny's route walking home from downtown, the same route he took every night he played. They were waiting for him in the dark. They murdered him, that's what I think."

He considered while she took a tissue out of her purse and dried her tears.

"Okay, but who would want to harm Danny? Does he have any enemies that you know of?"

She stared at him with her black penetrating eyes, remarkably composed under the circumstances. Again she paused. "So he owes a lotta people money around town, including his ex-wife Marci who's suing him for child support. Her new husband has threatened Danny more than once."

"Threatened him physically?"

"Yes."

He took a legal pad out of his desk and started taking notes. "What are their names? The ex-wife and her new husband?"

"Saenz. Richard and Marci Saenz. They live way out on Agua Fria Street."

"Anyone else?"

Oralia nodded. "I'm sure. We've both lived here a long time. Last week Danny got into a fight with drug dealers at a place they call Painted Skull Ranch up in Taos. Danny described it as some sort of guest ranch for dopers. His friend and mentor Dallas Longstreet has been hiding out there. Danny was supposed to open for Dallas at the Lensic this weekend, but Dallas unexpectedly cancelled. Friday morning Dallas walked out on his wife Belle at Bishop's Lodge Resort, where the two of them were staying. He told Danny he'd changed his mind and wouldn't be doing the concert. Dallas hasn't been seen in Santa Fe since."

"What about his wife? Is she still staying at Bishop's Lodge?"

She nodded. "I talked to her this morning. Do you know Dallas?"

"Sure, the country rock singer from Austin. He performs at least once a year in Santa Fe. I've seen him a couple of times over the years."

"Then you know Danny always opens for Dallas in Santa Fe and Taos," she responded. "In fact, Danny depends on a headliner like Dallas for a good part of his income, so he's been trying to persuade Dallas to leave this Painted Skull Ranch and start performing again. It's too late for the Lensic, but they have a concert in Taos next week. Danny was hoping to get Dallas clean for that."

Fernando sat back in his chair. "So Dallas is an addict? That's why he's at the ranch—to get drugs? Is that what you're saying?"

"Yes. And an alcoholic," Oralia said. "He goes off on these binges from time to time and it's hard to bring him back. Always before his band would take care of him, but this time he didn't bring the band. He and Danny were scheduled to perform acoustic sets on this tour."

"So who attacked Danny at this ranch? You say drug dealers, but can you be more specific?"

She shook her head. "I'm not sure. I haven't been there, but I know the drug dealer is an old friend of Dallas from Texas. He's been renting Painted Skull Ranch for a few months. Danny said he used to manage Dallas' band. He brought with him some of his friends. Apparently it was a couple of these guys who attacked Danny and told him not to come back. Danny didn't give me all the details—he was like that, not wanting to worry me."

"What's the name of this guy, the drug dealer?" Fernando asked.

"Travis Walker," she said. "Danny said the ranch is several miles east of Taos on Highway Sixty-four—just past Cañon at the edge of the National Forest. The way Danny described it, there's a long driveway off to the left marked by a totem pole at the entrance. Actually it's not a real totem pole, just the remainder of a tree trunk with a painted human skull on top. Which is why the place is called Painted Skull Ranch, I guess."

"Okay, let me see what I can find out and get back to you," Fernando said. "I'll contact the Taos County Sheriff first and then drive up to Taos. Maybe I'll also talk to the ex-wife and her husband, since Danny had an altercation with the new husband. If you think of anyone else Danny had issues with, let me know. Otherwise I'll call you if I have any more questions."

"Thank you."

"Oh, and here's my rate card." He opened his top desk drawer and handed her a card listing his retainer and hourly fees. "Don't worry about the money. We'll work something out."

A faint smile appeared on her moon face. "That's what Ruby said you'd say."

"You know Ruby?" he asked.

"Yeah, I'm a potter. I belong to her pottery co-op."

"I thought you looked familiar. That's where I've seen you."

She nodded, holding her belly with both hands and rising slowly out of her chair. She looked down at him. "Please find out who murdered Danny."

"I'll do my best," he said.

3

From the window Fernando watched Oralia walk to the parking lot and climb gingerly into her car, an old Honda Accord with dented fenders and a missing front bumper. He continued to watch as she drove off heading north on Canyon Road. Standing at the window he considered what she'd told him. He wanted to believe her story, but he needed more information about why the Santa Fe Police Department suspected a random encounter rather than a planned killing. He had to admit a random encounter sounded more plausible. Oralia's list of enemies seemed somewhat far-fetched, not to mention vague. A couple of amorphous drug dealers at a guest ranch in Taos?

To learn more he called his former colleague Manny Alvarez, now acting lead detective at the Washington Street station. "Fernando! Nice to hear from you, man! What's up?"

"I just need some information," Fernando said. "So how's everything down there? Are you getting along with the Chief?"

"Hah! I'm his whipping boy now that you're gone," Manny said. "He's driving me crazy!"

"Sounds familiar."

"Yeah, the Chief doesn't trust me," Manny continued. "He's bringing in a guy from Colorado Springs to take over as lead detective. Lots of experience, but he doesn't know a fucking thing about Santa Fe. Go figure."

"Another Anglo?"

'You got it, brother. So what information do you need? I'll see what I can do."

"On the Danny Ortiz homicide." Fernando waited for a response but none came. "Are you still there?"

"Yeah... but just between you and me, I'd stay away from the Ortiz case. Why are you interested?"

"His wife Oralia came to see me today," Fernando said. "She thinks Danny was set up."

Again, silence.

"So what can you tell me?" Fernando asked.

"Be careful, my friend," Manny said. "You might not like what you find."

"What do you mean? Is there a problem?"

"I'll tell you what. Meet me at the morgue in an hour and I'll show you the problem. Can you do that?"

"I'll be there," Fernando said.

While waiting he Googled Travis Walker, the name of the alleged drug dealer renting the ranch in Taos where Danny was attacked. He found several news articles in the *Austin American-Statesman* and the *Dallas Morning News* from a few years back. It turned out Walker was—or at least had been—a music agent and the manager of a country rock band called The Tumbleweeds, featuring none other than Dallas Longstreet. Most of the articles were about the band, their notoriously raucous tours and the various personalities on the band. The last article he found from three years ago in the *Dallas Morning News* reported that Walker had been sentenced to one-year probation for tax fraud connected to a dubious, self-proclaimed church that featured country and western music as gospel. After that, Walker disappeared from the web altogether, as though he had been transported to another planet.

The early articles ran alongside an identical photo of Walker showing a tall, ruggedly handsome man with dark hair and a close-cropped goatee. In the photo Walker wore a Western-style trimmed blue blazer over a white shirt and jeans. Hanging from his neck was a thick bolo tie with a turquoise stone the size of a golf ball. Living in Santa Fe Fernando had grown familiar with the attire, which he called the Santa Fe chic businessman look. From all appearances Walker looked like a professional wheeler-dealer.

His research begged the question: what had Travis Walker been doing over the last three years?

When it was time to go he locked up the office and drove out to Christus Saint Vincent Hospital on St. Michael's Drive. He left the Cherokee in the side parking lot and walked inside, taking the elevator down to the bottom floor. When the elevator door opened he stepped out into the cold tile corridor that was all too familiar. He walked down the long corridor to the morgue at the very end. When the automatic doors opened, he found Manny sitting in the front office with Miguel and Teresa, the main forensics team.

"Hey, Fernando, I'm surprised to see you here," Miguel greeted him.

"Hah! He can't stay away," Manny said. "After all these years he's addicted to the morgue!"

Fernando laughed. Sort of. "You invited me to meet you here, remember?"

"Don't pay any attention to these assholes," Teresa said. "How's retirement?"

"So far, so good. I decided to do a little private work and set up an office on Canyon Road. Stop by and check it out when you get a chance. I'll try it and see if I like the work. If not, I'll stay home and argue with Estelle all day."

They laughed.

Manny stood up. "Let me show you what I mean about the Ortiz case." He led them into the dissection room and stood back while Miguel opened a drawer that contained the body of Danny Ortiz.

Miguel pointed to Danny's face. "You can see the facial trauma where someone pummeled him, but the cause of death was asphyxiation. See the thumb marks on his neck there? We think death occurred sometime between ten and eleven p.m. Saturday night."

Fernando turned to Manny. "So what else do you know?"

"Well, first of all, we know he was attacked by two men. We found two sets of footprints in the wet grass. Apparently they were fighting with each other when Ortiz walked into the park on his way home. Then for some reason the two men attacked Ortiz. We think it was just a random encounter. Bad luck. Danny just happened to be in the wrong place at the wrong time. Maybe he even tried to stop the fight between the two assailants and they turned on him. Who knows?"

Fernando nodded. "And money was taken from Danny's wallet?"

"Yeah, they took the cash out and tossed the wallet on the grass," Manny said. "Could have been a couple of drunks on their way home...or maybe a couple of homeless people looking for a place to sleep the night."

"But they didn't take Danny's guitar, an expensive Les Paul Gibson," Fernando said. "That would bring some quick cash at any pawn shop. Maybe some serious cash."

"True," Manny said.

Fernando shook his head. "And Cathedral Park's not a place typically frequented by drunks or homeless people."

Manny shrugged. "Just speculating."

"Okay, but what about the possibility that Danny knew his attackers? That they were waiting for him in the park? It's worth investigating, isn't it?"

"No. Let me show you why."

Manny stepped up to the drawer and with Miguel's help turned Danny's left arm just enough to reveal dozens of scars from needle marks.

Fernando turned to Manny. "So?"

"So the Chief doesn't want to waste time on an addict, especially one found choked to death after fighting in a public park," Manny said. "To him it's a question of resources. He doesn't give a shit about addicts or drunks or anyone he considers scum of the earth. You know the Chief."

Teresa clucked her tongue. "He has a real attitude problem."

"What else is new?" Manny asked.

Fernando looked again at the needle marks and then turned to Miguel and Teresa. "How recent are these marks?"

Miguel shrugged. "Looks like a few are more recent, but most of the scar tissue is old. I'd say at least several months."

"Okay, thanks." He glanced at Manny. "I'll be in touch."

4

After leaving the morgue Fernando sat in his Cherokee for a good long while thinking. That Danny was ambushed seemed unlikely. Since when did hit men pummel and then choke their victims to death with their hands? On the other hand Cathedral Park was not a place where drunks or street people tended to congregate, making a random encounter seem equally unlikely. Something else bothered him even more: the needle marks on Danny's arm. Addicts brought nothing but trouble to themselves and everyone around them. The fact that Danny was, or had been, an addict opened up all sorts of possibilities, all of them bad.

Uncertain of his next move, he drove back to his office and found Ruby's Subaru parked next to her gallery. He and Ruby were old friends from the culture wars. He loved Ruby, although she could be prickly. Her in-your-face personality put off many people but had made her a force in Santa Fe politics for over two decades. A potter by trade, Ruby had risen through the ranks of *La Raza* to become the most progressive member of City Council ever. Back in the 1990s she fought tooth and nail with all the greedy developers who wanted to turn downtown Santa Fe into one big shopping mall. She led rallies, marches, protests, sit-ins, and if you believed the rumors, a fire-bombing or two.

She lost, of course. The developers and the Sotheby's crowd turned Santa Fe into Disneyland Southwest. The tide of gentrification sweeping over Santa Fe during those years hollowed out the city. Gone were most of the people whose families had lived in Santa Fe for generations. Ever higher home values and property taxes priced out all who couldn't afford million dollar homes. After two tumultuous terms on City Council lecturing, berating, cajoling, and threatening the other members, she said 'fuck it' and retired to the pottery co-op she owned and ran with a number of other potters, all of them women.

Still, she refused to be silenced. She made it a point to attend most Council meetings and give the members a piece of her mind. Every one of them feared Ruby's tirades. Occasionally her anger would get the better of her language and she would be asked to leave. Once a few years back City Council banned her for the year, but her lawyer, Raoul Garcia, sued their asses and got her reinstated in her front row seat staring down the Council. Since then she'd continued to raise hell.

Ruby had inherited the Canyon Road studio from her ex-husband, Jimmy Mackey. Jimmy was a painter with a modest reputation in Santa Fe and northern New Mexico who was murdered last year in a raunchy sex scandal involving a host of Canyon Road artists as well as the then mayor of Santa Fe and his estranged wife. Fortunately for Fernando, the studio came with a detached garage that needed an occupant. Since he needed an office, the arrangement worked well for both of them.

Fernando climbed the steps to Ruby's gallery and opened the door. The walls where Jimmy's paintings once hung were now lined with wooden shelves. On the shelves colorful ceramics from Ruby's pottery co-op were displayed. She'd kept Jimmy's small kitchen off to the side but turned his bedroom into an office. A few small paintings of Jimmy's hung on the back wall. He could hear Ruby cursing as he stepped into the spacious front room.

"Jesus Christ! I don't have time for this. Look at me! I look like a washer woman! Oh...Fernando! You scared me!" she said, coming out of her office.

"Sorry, Ruby. I should have rung the bell."

"Nah. No problem. I'm just frustrated," Ruby said. "I need somebody here when I'm at the co-op and vice versa. I can't be in both places at the same time, you know? And look at me! Do I look like I should be on the floor of a gallery selling fine art?"

He laughed. She wore her usual potting clothes: jeans, blue work shirt, and a red bandana tied around her head. The bandana kept her curly black hair from spilling down across her face, which was smudged with gray clay from her potter's wheel. As were her clothes.

"And the tourist season is about to begin," she said, shaking her head. "I need to clean up my act. Plus, I don't even have a name for the new gallery yet. I'm thinking of naming it Three Cities of Spain, after the old restaurant on Canyon Road."

"Not bad. We used to love that restaurant. Might bring you luck."

Ruby nodded. "You think?"

"And why not ask the women at the co-op to help out at the gallery?" Fernando asked. "They could take shifts. You don't charge them much for their spaces at the co-op, so why not? Their pots are sold here too."

"Yeah, maybe. That's not a bad idea," Ruby said. "Some of the gals don't clean up too good, though, but I guess that's okay. Most of the dumb-ass tourists who come in here don't look any better."

He walked into the kitchen, separated from the front room by a new marble countertop. Ruby had kept a couple of Jimmy's "Chopped Nudes" paintings hanging on the kitchen walls. Nude women with appendages and orifices protruding from various body parts, splashed with bright colors. Supposed to be similar to some of Pablo Picasso's paintings.

"I see you've kept some of Jimmy's paintings," he said.

"Yeah, I owe him that much, the bastard. So are you all settled in down there in the garage?"

"Pretty much," Fernando said. "Oralia Ortiz stopped by and wants me to find out who killed Danny."

"Good. I told her to come see you. The whole thing sounds fishy to me," Ruby said.

"Oralia mentioned the husband of Danny's ex-wife as someone who'd physically threatened him...and some thugs at a place called Painted Skull Ranch in Taos where Dallas Longstreet has been staying. You know, the county rock singer from Austin who comes through Santa Fe every year."

Ruby nodded. "Sure, I know Dallas. I can't say he's a friend, but I met him through Danny years ago."

"What about this Travis Walker, the guy who's renting the ranch?" Fernando asked. Apparently he's calling the place a rustic guest ranch. He used to manage Dallas' band."

"I met him once or twice, back in the day," Ruby said, frowning. "He wasn't one of my favorite people, to put it mildly."

"Is he a drug dealer?"

"Travis? Could be. He and Dallas used to shoot up together. Travis was into some pretty dark shit."

"Like what?" he asked.

"Well, drugs and kinky sex mostly. He tried to hit on me once, hands all over my ass. I told him to go fuck himself."

He relayed what Oralia had told him: that Danny needed money and had been trying to persuade Dallas to leave Painted Skull Ranch and get back on tour, for which he had been kicked off the ranch by a couple of tough guys and told not to return. Whether Dallas was choosing to stay at the ranch or being held against his will was anyone's guess.

"Both sound plausible," Ruby said. "Dallas will do anything for drugs. On the other hand Travis likes to control Dallas. That's why they broke up when Travis managed the band. He's a control freak."

He nodded.

She turned and looked around the gallery. "Jesus, I gotta clean up," she said, changing the topic. "You never know when some rich Texan will wander in and want to buy some hippie pottery."

Fernando turned to go and then stopped and looked at Ruby. "Hey, I could take a shift or two if you want to line up people to staff the gallery. You know, to compensate for free rent."

She laughed. "No way! You look even worse than I do!"

5

Fernando waited until half past six before driving out Agua Fria to visit Danny's ex-wife and her new husband, Richard and Marci Saenz. He found the address, a small L-shaped adobe with a dirt lawn. Two small kids played outside, a girl riding a tricycle hell-bent down the sidewalk and an older boy with a skateboard rolling up and down the slanted drive. He parked on the street, dodged the kid on the tricycle, and walked across the dirt to the front door. He heard a television inside, some news or talk show where different speakers were arguing about something. He rang the doorbell and stood back on the porch, admiring the blue trim around the door and windows that kept out evil spirits according to New Mexico legend.

Eventually a smallish woman wearing workout tights and a sleeveless tank top came to the door. She looked younger than Danny, maybe early forties and athletic with her hair fixed in a tight bun on top of her head. She stared at him suspiciously for a second and then asked, "Yeah, what do you want?"

"Mrs. Saenz, my name is Fernando Lopez. I'm a private eye investigating your ex-husband's death? Do you mind if I ask you a few questions?"

She looked him over, frowning. Then she opened the door for him and without saying a word turned and walked into the house. He followed, closing the door behind him. They entered a living room where she grabbed the TV remote and turned off the television. She pointed to a beat-up beige sofa that looked as though the kids used it as a trampoline. She sat across the room from him in a matching beige chair and stared at him, waiting.

"Sorry for your loss—" he started, but she cut him off.

"Not my loss," she said. "It's the kids' loss. They won't be getting any more child support."

"You know Danny was murdered, right?" Fernando asked.

She nodded.

"Did he have any enemies?"

"I suppose, but no one who would murder him. Except me!" she said, laughing. "I'm joking, I hope you understand."

Fernando smiled. "What about your husband? Didn't he and Danny argue about child support?"

She shot him a dirty look. "Hah! Don't tell me you suspect Richard! He and Danny might have argued a time or two, but that's all! Both of them are pussies! Neither of them could hurt a flea if he tried!"

"So where was Richard Saturday night about ten p.m.?"

She sighed. "He works the three to eleven shift at Christus Saint Vincent Hospital. He's an orderly. His only days off are Wednesday and Thursday. Call them if you don't believe me. Okay?"

He watched her carefully, trying to get a read. "At what time did he come home Saturday night?"

"The same time he always comes home, between eleven thirty and eleven forty-five," she said, showing her impatience.

Suddenly she stood up from the sofa. "That's all I know. The only contact I've had with Danny over the past three years is trying to get him to pay child support. Which hasn't been easy. Understand?"

He followed her to the front door, not about to give up just yet. "Was Danny shooting drugs when you were married?"

She stopped and stared at him. "Yeah. On and off. That's why I divorced him. He would start and then go to the clinic and get clean for a while and then start again. I couldn't take it any more. I threw him out. There's noting worse than living with a fucking addict!"

Just then the smaller of the two kids came running up to the door bawling. "Mommy...Sammy ran into me and knocked me off my tricycle! My leg is bleeding!"

Marci turned to him. "Look, I gotta go. I have nothing else to say."

"Much obliged," he said, stepping around the crying child. He climbed into his Cherokee and sat there for a while watching the western sky darken. He made a mental note to call Christus Saint Vincent to find out if by any chance Richard had left work early Saturday night. Even so, it would be tight. It would have taken Richard at least twenty or thirty minutes to get downtown, park, and walk into Cathedral Park. Then he would have to meet up with a second assailant somewhere. Two guys had attacked Danny, not one.

Plus, it didn't make any sense for Richard to murder Danny, when he and his wife counted on Danny for child support. It just didn't figure.

He checked his watch. It was already past seven. He was late for dinner, which meant that Estelle would be pissed again. He could hear her: "You're supposed to be retired, remember?"

Even so, Fernando decided to make one stop on what was turning out to be a long, tiring day. He drove back to the Paseo and then around to Otero Street. Halfway up the hill he found the duplex where Oralia lived. It was a plain cinderblock building with a flat tin roof. There was a 'For Rent' sign in the patch of weeds that served as a front yard. He supposed that meant the other half of the shabby duplex was for rent, not Oralia's half.

He parked on the broken concrete of the driveway and walked to the porch. He heard voices inside as he knocked on the door. A moment later the door opened. Oralia froze, surprised to see him.

"Sorry to bother you so late," Fernando said. "I didn't expect you to have company."

"Oh...a couple of friends came over to help out." She didn't invite him to come inside.

He could see two women in the kitchen directly behind Oralia. They were chatting and drinking glasses of wine.

"I'll be quick," he said. "Did you know Danny had been shooting drugs?"

She sighed. "I knew he'd been addicted before we were married. I was worried he would start again. That's why I didn't want him to go to Taos."

"Could drugs be why he was killed?"

"How do you mean?" she asked.

"Stealing drugs? Selling drugs?"

"I don't know. He was always so secretive, never telling me where he was going or what he was doing. Used to drive me crazy. We only married because I got pregnant. It was a mistake. Everything."

He waited for her to continue.

"Listen, I just want to know who murdered him," she said. "For closure. Do you understand?"

He didn't but nodded his head anyway.

6

After breakfast next morning Fernando deliberately waited until right before Estelle left for work before telling her about his new client and that he needed to drive up to Taos that morning. She turned, halfway out the front door, and gave him the Evil Eye. She didn't have time to give him a proper scolding because she was running late for her job at the Saint Francis Outreach Program, which provided food and clothing and services to the growing immigrant community in Santa Fe, a sanctuary city. That, of course, was why he waited until the last minute to tell her.

He and Estelle had been at odds since he'd retired earlier that year. Estelle wanted him to stay in Santa Fe and do divorce or insurance work, something safe and close to home. Try as he might he couldn't make her understand that he didn't control who walked into his office or what kind of problems they wanted him to solve. Not only that, but having just started his business as a private investigator he didn't have the leisure of turning away clients.

So as soon as Estelle drove off in her Camry, Fernando grabbed his holster, his binoculars, and a thermos of coffee and walked outside to his Cherokee. He drove down sleepy Acequia Madre to the Paseo and around to the entrance to Highway 285 North. The bright, clear morning cheered him as he passed the Tesuque turnoff and the Santa Fe Opera. Coming into Pojoaque he saw the hazy blue Jemez Mountains in the distance. In Española he turned north on Highway 68 to Taos, a straight shot north to the high country.

Known as the Low Road to Taos, Highway 68 ran alongside the Rio Grande as it snaked its way through the river valley. To either side of the river piñon and juniper trees pock-marked the triangular hills. Just past Dixon he began to see brightly colored kayaks and white water rafts bobbing and splashing on their way down the river. Approaching the parking areas near Velarde he saw trailers belonging to the commercial rafting companies parked side by side on the gravel lots. Several rafts were in the process of launching. Two rafters wearing orange life jackets and helmets waved at him as he drove by on the highway. He ignored them.

Fernando drove around the last sweeping curve and then up the hill to the Taos plateau and into the community of Ranchos de Taos. He slowed down driving past the famous church, painted and photographed by Georgia O'Keeffe and a zillion other artists. Ahead the ribbon of highway ran straight to the 13,000-foot Taos Mountains on the far horizon. He ignored the cheap motels, gas stations, and convenience stores cluttering both sides of the road. Nearing the central Plaza area he turned right onto Albright and then right again onto Lovato Place. Then he pulled into a parking place behind the Taos County Sherriff's Office, a concrete and steel building that looked more like a warehouse than an office.

Instead of calling, he'd decided to stop by the sheriff's office on his way into Taos. He knew the sheriff, Hank Mathews, from his days as lead detective at the Santa Fe Police Department. They'd worked together on a couple of high profile cases, including the kidnapping and murder of a well-known Santa Fe historian and podcaster. He liked Hank, a crusty old dog who always wore his dirty black Stetson and carried a heavy .44 magnum Colt. Old Hank was getting a little prickly in his old age, but who the hell wasn't?

He climbed out of the Cherokee and walked into the office.

"Hey, Fernando," the woman behind the counter said. "Don't tell me another Santa Fean has been kidnapped in Taos?"

He laughed. "Not exactly, Sally. This time I'm looking for a missing musician. From Austin, Texas. Is Hank available?"

Sally shook her head. "Hasn't come in yet this morning. He's been keeping irregular hours since his wife died a few months ago. Should be here soon if you want to wait."

So he took a seat in the waiting room and chatted with Sally, a tiny young woman with tattoos on her arms and black hair tied back in one long braid.

A few minutes later Hank walked through the door grumbling about something. He looked a bit disheveled, as though he'd had a hard night. He perked up when he saw Fernando sitting in the waiting room.

"Well I'll be! Must be trouble in Dodge!" Hank said. "What brings you up to Taos, Fernando?"

Fernando laughed. "Just need some information. Thought I would stop by and say hello. That seemed like the personable thing to do."

"Well, hell, come on back." Hank led the way down the hall and into his corner office overlooking the parking lot. He hung his Stetson on a coat rack and sat down behind his desk.

"You doing okay?" Fernando asked, taking a chair.

"Yeah, thanks to the cooks at Michael's Kitchen...and my daughter, who comes over to help me now and again," Hank said. "Ain't been easy since Esther died. Like I've told you before, I'm a piss poor cook and not much for keeping house. I'm better with the yard, but even there I depended on Esther to give me orders. Otherwise I forget what the hell needs to be done and when it needs to be done. Pathetic how much a man depends on the women in his life."

"No doubt about it," Fernando said. "I don't know what I'd do without Estelle to keep me on the strait and narrow."

"Hah! I'll tell you what! You'd be sittin' right here complaining about cooking and cleaning house, just like me!" Hank roared, slapping the top of the desk with his open hand.

Fernando laughed.

"Hank squinted, giving him the Evil Eye. "So why are you here?"

"Well, it's complicated," Fernando said.

"Ain't it always," Hank replied.

"Seems a local musician was murdered last weekend in Santa Fe. You might have read about him, Danny Ortiz. His wife hired me to find the killer. Danny was scheduled to perform in Santa Fe and Taos with Dallas Longstreet, the country rock singer from Austin. But Longstreet bailed at the last minute and took off to a place called Painted Skull Ranch east of Taos on Highway Sixty-four."

Hank looked puzzled. "So? It's a free country, ain't it?"

"Well, I'm told the ranch is being rented by a friend of Dallas who happens to be a drug dealer," Fernando said. "Danny's wife thinks the ranch is some sort of drug house holding Longstreet captive, because when Danny went up to Taos and tried to spring Longstreet, he got into a fight with a couple of thugs who manhandled him and kicked him off the property."

Hank threw up his hands. "What the hell are you saying? You think this drug dealer and his goons killed your musician down in Santa Fe?"

"Don't know," Fernando said. "I'm here to check out the ranch and try to speak with Dallas Longstreet. I wondered if you knew anything about the ranch or the drug dealer."

"Whereabouts is it?" Hank asked.

"Like I said, it's east of Taos on Highway Sixty-four, just past Cañon."

"Hmmm...they might call it Painted Skull Ranch now, but that sounds like the old Candelaria Hacienda," Hank said. "It's almost as old as the Martinez House, nearly two hundred years."

Hank spun around to face his computer and hit a few keys. "Yeah...

we've had a few complaints in the last couple of months. Mostly about noise and drunkenness...erratic behavior...that sort of thing. Nothing that would warrant a citation. Hell, if we gave citations for wild behavior, half the folks in Taos would be in jail!"

"Anything else?"

Hank shook his head. "So who's the drug dealer?"

"Guy by the name of Travis Walker, also from Austin," Fernando said. "He used to manage Dallas Longstreet's band. Something of a con-man, I'm told."

Hank frowned. "Never heard of him, but I figure he must rent the ranch from Bill Candelaria Bill's the last surviving descendant of the Candelaria family. Lives up in Pueblo. I haven't seen old Bill in over a year."

Fernando nodded. "Okay, thanks for the information. I'm going to head out there now and have a look around. I wanted to stop by and talk to you first. See if you knew anything about the ranch.

"Well, let me know what you find," Hank said. "If this Travis Walker is running a drug house, I could get interested fast."

7

After leaving Hank's office Fernando sat for a moment in his Cherokee brooding. He had no idea how to approach Travis Walker...or how to get into the ranch. He considered his options, none of them particularly good. Finally he decided to freelance, to just show up and see what transpired. So he pulled out on the highway and followed the stream of cars into Taos. At the Plaza he turned right onto Kit Carson Road and drove by the famous Mabel Dodge Luhan House on Morada Lane. Beyond the city limits Kit Carson became Highway 64, which would take him all the way to Angel Fire and Cimarron.

Just before Cañon he spotted the totem pole Oralia had told him about. It stood on the left side of the highway marking the entrance to Painted Skull Ranch. In reality the totem pole was a tree stump with what looked like a real human skull with painted red eye sockets on top. That surprised him. You didn't often see a human skull used as a sign or a warning or whatever it was supposed to be. He knew it wasn't necessarily illegal to possess a human skull, unless it was Native American or illegally obtained, but still? What was the point?

Mystified, he drove past the entrance hoping to get a better view of the property. From the entrance he could only see an ocotillo branch fence with a scattering of flat roofs beyond. So he continued on for another hundred yards or so until a series of gradually rising bluffs completely blocked his view. So he turned around and drove back to the totem pole with the human skull on top.

Fernando proceeded slowly down the gravel drive, still not sure what he was going to say when he arrived at the ranch. Further down the drive he approached the ocotillo branch fence, which ran along the front of the house and blocked the view. An opening in the fence served as a gate, so he eased through the opening into a gravel parking lot. Several vehicles were parked on one side of the lot, including an old Ford pickup with rusted fenders and a sky blue Cadillac CT5 with Texas license plates that read LSTREET. He parked on the opposite side of the lot next to what was left of a flagstone walkway and set the brake on the Cherokee.

He studied the lay of the land as soon as he climbed out of the Cherokee. To his right the massive Candelaria hacienda looked like a museum. Built with thick adobe walls and arched buttresses, it showed every bit of its two hundred years. The uneven walls sagged in places and bulged in others. Entire patches of the brown stucco had crumbled, revealing straw and mud bricks underneath. The flat tin roof had rusted to a brownish red, while the unpainted windowsills had faded to a dark gray. The heavy front door hung on enormous metal hinges that matched the door handle. Someone had painted a skull and crossbones in red paint on the wooden door. What the hell? Was that supposed to match the red-eyed skull at the front entrance? Someone here had a fetish for skulls and red paint.

From the parking lot Fernando walked straight ahead on the broken fragments of flagstone. The walkway took him into a courtyard between the hacienda and a scattering of smaller adobe structures to his left. The first of the small buildings had collapsed inward, revealing a stone fireplace and a series of anvils and metal tools that told him it had been a *herreria*, a blacksmith shop. The second building, also collapsed, may have been a *carpinteria*. Beyond the first two adobes he saw a scattering of smaller buildings, all shoddily constructed frame bungalows that may have housed the manual laborers who once worked on the estate. In the center of the courtyard was a raised bank of hollyhocks and rose bushes overrun with weeds.

Then he saw the morada at the end of the courtyard and stopped. The small adobe church had the traditional bell tower at one end of the roof and a wooden cross at the other, with its cemetery behind and off to one side. Its outer walls were cracked and its adobe buttresses were crumbling, but the rectangular structure was still standing after nearly two centuries. The presence of a morada meant the hacienda and its immediate neighborhood had its own Penitente Brotherhood, a lay religious organization related to the Catholic Church popular in northern New Mexico. Before he had time to investigate he heard footsteps approaching behind him. Someone was walking down from the house to join him.

"Hi there. Are you looking for someone?"

Fernando turned to find a tall gangly man with long stringy red hair carrying a basket filled with bed sheets and towels. Given his disheveled look, he could have been anywhere between thirty and sixty years old.

"Oh hi," Fernando said in the friendliest voice he could muster. "Yeah, I heard the country musician Dallas Longstreet is staying here. I'm a big fan and wondered if I might say hello."

"Sure, I guess," the man said timidly and laid down his basket.

Fernando smiled. "Who are you, if you don't mind me asking?"

"I'm Jerry, the caretaker," the man said. "I'm also the housekeeper, groundskeeper, and anything else Mister Walker wants me to be. He's my boss."

"Is Mister Walker here?" Fernando asked.

The man shook his head. "No, they drove down to Albuquerque this morning. They're meeting the Southwest Chief at the Amtrak station there. Picking up a shipment from L.A."

Fernando nodded.

"Anyway, let me show you the way. I think Mister Longstreet is on the porch with Jenny."

Fernando followed Jerry around behind the house to a rickety porch with a wooden pergola for a roof. Heavy vines on the pergola blocked out the sun and offered shade. As he approached he saw Dallas Longstreet sitting in a cane-backed rocking chair strumming an acoustic guitar. Dallas resembled legendary singer Jerry Jeff Walker so much that the two of them could have been twins. Up close he looked even older than his fifty-some years: a tan, wrinkled face with a gray cowlick across his forehead. He wore an embroidered western shirt, jeans, concho belt, and snakeskin boots. His uniform onstage and off.

Then Fernando noticed another person on the porch, a big-haired woman wearing a short skirt and halter top. She sat on a wooden bench humming a tune. She seemed to be accompanying Dallas.

"Mister Longstreet, this here's a big fan of yours," Jerry said. "He wanted to stop by and say hello, if it's alright with you."

Dallas turned his head to look at them, eyes glazed. "Who?"

Jerry looked nervous, as if realizing he'd made a big mistake. "Well...I guess you know your way out," he said to Fernando and walked away, returning to his basket of laundry.

"Fernando Lopez," he introduced himself to Dallas and then leaned against the porch railing. "I wanted to let you know that Danny Ortiz was murdered in Santa Fe last Saturday, in case you didn't know."

Dallas tried to focus his eyes. "Danny? Nooooo..."

"His wife thinks a couple of the guys who work for Travis Walker murdered Danny," Fernando said. "Maybe the guys who got into a fight with Danny up here when he came to see you? Do you remember?"

"Who?" Dallas looked around and spotted the woman on the bench.

"Oh...this pretty lil' thing is Jenny...she's a damn fine singer."

Fernando looked at the big-haired woman whose ratted-out hair appeared electrified. The teased blond hair resembled a halo. She must have been in her mid-forties, a bit too old for a skirt that short.

"Listen," Fernando said. "Do you want to get out of here? I have my car outside. I can give you a ride to Santa Fe."

Dallas shook his head and said, "Nah...I like it here. Me and Jenny, we got something goin'. Ain't that right, Jenny?"

"Damn straight," she said.

Fernando didn't believe him but said nothing.

Dallas turned to Jenny. "Yeah...let's sing some old-time cowboy songs, Jenny. How 'bout 'Don't Fence Me In'?"

Jenny waved him away with a swat of her hand. The two of them were totally zonked. "Ah, give me something romantic, daddy," she said. "I know."

With that Jenny burst out singing: "From this valley they say you are leaving..."

Dallas strummed his acoustic guitar and then joined her on the chorus: "Then come sit by my side if you love me / Do not hasten to bid me adieu / Just remember the Red River Valley / And the cowboy that's loved you so true."

Fernando didn't waste any more time asking questions. He checked the whereabouts of Jerry, who he saw carrying his basket of towels and sheets into one of the bungalows.

He waited until Jerry disappeared into the bungalow and closed the door behind him. Then Fernando climbed up on the porch and walked by Dallas and Jenny to the back screen door. He opened the door and stepped inside a large sparingly furnished room where he found a shepherd's fireplace along one wall. Instead of a mantle, the fireplace had a stone ledge where a shepherd—or anyone else—could sleep above the fire to stay warm on cold winter nights.

The walls of the room were pockmarked with *nichos* carved out of the adobe, each holding a *bulto* wood carving of a saint or another religious figure. In the largest niche he saw the carved skeleton of *la muerte* carrying a bow and arrow and dragging his death cart. Next to the small windows on either side of the room hung Navajo rugs, gray with black and red stripes. On the far wall a motley elk's head with an impressive rack of antlers gazed down mournfully on the meager furnishings: a small table with three chairs and a Taos bed. Not very well appointed for what was supposed to be a guest ranch. But then Fernando didn't see many guests.

Halfway across the room Fernando felt his shoes sticking to the floor and realized he was walking on a packed clay floor. The clay hadn't been polished in years. Once common in northern New Mexico, clay floors had all but disappeared from New Mexico homes. The last clay floor he remembered seeing had been in Georgia O'Keeffe's Abiquiu home, now a museum.

He walked under the ratty elk's head and into a hallway with tiny rooms off to either side. With just enough room for a single bed and bedside table, the rooms resembled the cells of a monastery. He found the first two bedrooms empty but the third occupied by a young man wearing bicycling clothing sitting up in bed with his eyes wide open staring off into space. He was either stoned or stone cold dead, Fernando couldn't tell which.

Fernando knocked on the side of the open door.

The young man's eyes fluttered and then closed.

Fernando walked over to the bed and asked, "Hey, man, are you okay?"

The young man nodded without opening his eyes.

Fernando noticed a plastic bag containing several blue pills on the bedside table. Looked like illegal fentanyl from Mexico. He took one of the tablets and dropped it in his shirt pocket. Then he asked, "Do you need help?"

The young man shook his head.

"Okay then," Fernando said, leaving the comatose biker and continuing on down the hallway. He passed a larger room with a locked door, probably Travis Walker's office. He thought about opening the door with his lock pick but then decided against it. He had no idea when Travis Walker and his hired hands would return. Why press his luck?

He walked to the end of the hall, entering a rustic kitchen with an open hearth built of massive stones blackened from decades of use. Heavy cast-iron fixtures and pots and pans hung from exposed vigas on the ceiling. A long picnic table with benches on either side took up most of the wall opposite the fireplace. The charred remains of a recent fire spilled over the andiron in the center of the fireplace. The smell of smoke lingered in the air.

Fernando paused before opening the front door, debating whether he should leave now or wait for Travis to return. He decided to leave because didn't feel like confronting Travis Walker quite yet. He needed more time to think.

Clearly, Dallas wouldn't be of much help--unless he managed to detox fast, which wasn't likely to happen as long as he remained at the ranch.

Maybe Dallas' wife could persuade him to leave the ranch and get clean.

Fernando didn't see any other possibility. That meant a trip to Bishop's Lodge Resort in Santa Fe where she was staying, according to Oralia.

Now that he had a plan Fernando opened the door a crack to make sure the coast was clear. It was, or so he thought.

8

Once outside Fernando followed the flagstone path up a small rise to the gravel parking lot. Only when he neared the top did he see them. Travis and two of his men leaned against the front of the Cherokee waiting for him. Their sleek Audi, gray with darkly tinted windows, was parked behind the Cherokee blocking his exit. Fernando swallowed. Looked like he would have to confront Travis now after all, whether he wanted to or not.

"You a cop?" Travis asked. The man was just as handsome in person as he was in his photographs. Tall, muscular, with close-cropped dark hair and goatee, he wore a clean white shirt and dark jeans and sunglasses.

"Private investigator," Fernando said. He couldn't help but notice the open carry holsters worn by the other two men, beefy types dressed in western shirts and jeans. All of them wore dark sunglasses.

"What are you investigating?" Travis asked.

"The wife of Danny Ortiz hired me to find his killers. My name's Fernando Lopez."

"So why are you here? Ortiz was killed in Santa Fe, yes?"

"Danny's wife said he got into a fight with two of your men up here," Fernando said. "Maybe these two?"

Travis sighed. "Not a fight. My men had to escort him off the property because he was disturbing our guests. We can't have that. Our guests come here to relax...and to get away from people like Ortiz. And you."

"What about Dallas Longstreet?" Fernando asked. "Is he here to relax, or are you holding him against his will."

Travis laughed. He turned to his men. "He thinks we're holding Dallas here against his will." The other two laughed.

"Dallas can come and go whenever he wants," Travis said. "My guess is that you've already talked with him. Did he seem like he wanted to go with you? Or with anyone else, for that matter?"

Fernando shrugged. "He wasn't in any shape to do anything. As I'm sure you know."

"Let me tell you something, Mr. private investigator," Travis said. "Dallas Longstreet is a friend of mine. I've known him for over twenty years. I used to manage his band. So for you to come up here and accuse me of kidnapping him doesn't set well with me. In fact, I consider that downright unfriendly. An insult." He turned to his men. "What do you guys think?"

"I think he needs to be taught a lesson," the beefiest of the two shot back, a big man with a huge belly and legs as big around as tree trunks.

"I think we can oblige," the other man said.

"Good," Travis said and started down the hill toward the house. Then he stopped and looked back at Fernando. "And don't come back."

Fernando watched Travis walk away. When the two men on top advanced, he moved. He headed up the walk toward the parking lot. When he did the beefy man stepped in front of him.

Fernando sidestepped the big man, who jostled him with his shoulder. The other man cursed and went to the Audi and opened the trunk. When he turned around he had a metal baseball bat in his hand.

Looking straight ahead, Fernando hurried to the Cherokee and climbed inside. He started the engine and stomped on the accelerator as the two men rushed to stop him.

The guy with the bat swung hard as the Cherokee took off. The bat shattered the backseat window on the right side of the Cherokee, spraying the inside of the vehicle with glass fragments.

The Cherokee fishtailed and then lurched forward over the lip of the hill nearly hitting the big man, who dove out of the way and rolled in the dirt. Spinning around in a semi-circle, the Cherokee showered the two men with dirt and flagstone fragments. For a split second Fernando thought the tires of the Cherokee would sink in the sandy hillside, but he cranked the steering wheel hard to the right and felt the four-wheel-drive kick in. The Cherokee bounced back over the lip of the hill and shot off fast into the parking lot. The Cherokee raced across the parking lot into the driveway, kicking up gravel as it went. At the junction of Highway 64 Fernando slowed to a stop and then turned right toward town.

All the way into Taos Fernando kept checking the rear-view mirror for any sign of the Audi. He saw none.

Once he came to the Plaza and turned south on Highway 68 he started to breath easier. The line of tourist vehicles coming into town stretched out as far as the eye could see. Cars, vans, and RVs were lined up all the way from the Plaza to Ranchos de Taos. He thanked his lucky stars that he was going the other direction. Beyond Pilar he began to relax for real, with the high sandstone cliffs on his left and the Rio Grande River on his right.

Fernando stopped at a Wendy's in Española for a quick lunch. He went inside to break up the long drive and ate his sandwich in a corner booth. While he ate he took the blue pill out of his shirt pocket and turned it over in his hand. No markings. It was identical to all the others he'd become accustomed to seeing over the last few years: bootleg fentanyl from Mexico or Central America. Illegal fentanyl entered the country from border cities like El Paso, Nogales, and San Diego and then spread its tentacles across the country.

He reflected on the changes in the illegal drug trade he'd witnessed over his thirty years of detective work. When he first started at the SFPD cocaine was the drug that created their biggest problems. If, that is, you didn't count marijuana, which had always been ubiquitous, legal or illegal; and if you disregarded heroin, which only a few high-rollers had the wherewithal to imbibe. Cocaine was followed in time by meth and now opioids. He could understand, sort of, using cocaine or meth for a short burst of energy, but why would anyone want to render themselves comatose by taking fentanyl? Zombies. He didn't get it. Never had.

By the time he finished his lunch and climbed back into the Cherokee he knew exactly where he was going next. Before getting back on the road he took out his cell phone and called Bishop's Lodge Resort in Santa Fe and asked to speak to Mrs. Dallas Longstreet. The operator put him on hold. Seconds later a friendly voice came over the phone. The voice seemed younger than what he expected Belle Longstreet would sound like.

"This is Paula, Belle Longstreet's assistant," the voice said. "Belle's not here at the moment. Can I help you?"

"I hope so," Fernando said.

9

Fernando took the first Tesuque exit off Highway 285. He drove quickly through the pricey, picture-perfect village where shacks could cost a million dollars and change. Bishop's Lodge Resort anchored the eastern edge of Tesuque, just down the hill from Santa Fe. The 400-acre property had an illustrious history, first purchased in the 1860s by Archbishop Jean Baptiste Lamy, the subject of Willa Cather's novel *Death Comes for the Archbishop*. Lamy built a chapel on the grounds and used it as a retreat. The lodge itself dated from the 1920s but last year had been remodeled and greatly expanded to accommodate what the owners referred to as the "luxury traveler," by which they meant the filthy rich. Rooms and casitas at the upscaled lodge ran upwards of one thousand dollars a night.

Fernando frowned as he turned into the driveway. The proverbial money changers had entered the temple. Archbishop Lamy must be turning over in his dusty grave.

He followed the outer loop around to the Cottonwood Casita, following Paula's directions. He pulled up behind a sky blue Cadillac Escalade that matched the CT5 he'd seen at Painted Skull Ranch. Matching cars, his and hers, ain't that sweet. He walked through an elaborate garden up to the veranda and knocked on the front door. Moments later a young woman with brown hair cut in a bob appeared on the other side of the glass. She smiled and opened the door wide.

"Please, come in," she said.

Paula wore black slacks and a tight white blouse. Early thirties, he figured. She seemed almost happy to see him, incredibly cheerful. Not the kind of person he usually encountered in his business.

Fernando stepped into the casita and stopped to admire the exquisitely furnished house with Southwestern décor throughout, everything from Navajo patterned upholstery on the furniture to kiva fireplaces in the corners and vigas on the ceilings. Navajo rugs and Georgia O'Keeffe inspired paintings hung on the walls, everything new and shiny and inviting. The kind of place that could almost make you happy for spending a thousand or two a night for a bed and a place to sleep. He saw a kitchen and multiple bedrooms off the front sitting room. In the sitting room a full bar occupied most of one wall. Next to the bar a door opened onto an enclosed patio complete with wrought iron furniture and brightly colored umbrellas. The works.

Paula noticed him looking at the bar. "Can I get you a cocktail? Maybe a gin and tonic? I'm also the house bartender."

Fernando laughed. "No, it's a bit too early for me, I'm afraid."

Paula laughed too. "I know what you mean. These people drink all day, from morning till night. I don't know how they do it."

They sat on sofas facing each other, neither of them speaking.

Finally Fernando spoke. "Where is Mrs. Longstreet?"

"Oh, she's off riding at the stables here. Belle loves horses. Actually, I think she prefers horses to people," Paula said, laughing again.

Fernando nodded, not sure of what to make of her friendliness. "Do you know if Missus Longstreet has spoken to her husband since he's been up in Taos? The reason I ask is that Danny Ortiz's wife said Danny told her that Dallas is being held against his will."

She shook her head "I don't think so. At least not to my knowledge. Only through their lawyers."

"What do you mean?" Fernando asked.

"Well, they're divorcing. Rather, she's divorcing him."

"Really?" Fernando asked, confused. "So why are they traveling together?"

Paula laughed. "Well...she's afraid he'll spend or give away their money. So she goes with him everywhere to keep an eye on him and their money. Until they finalize the papers."

"But he's in Taos now and she's still here."

"Yeah, go figure," Paula said. "He just took off Friday morning before she could stop him. Although, come to think about it, she really didn't try that hard to stop him."

Just then they heard what sounded like a golf cart pull up outside the casita. Someone said something outside and then the golf cart drove away. Seconds later the front door opened and in walked a tall, big-boned woman with an aristocratic flair. She wore a black show jacket over a white shirt and riding breeches with half chap. Boots and a riding helmet completed her outfit. She looked as though she'd been at a formal horse show.

"Belle, this is Fernando Lopez," Paula said to the tall woman. "He's a detective investigating Danny's murder."

"Private investigator," Fernando said, correcting Paula.

Belle ripped off her riding helmet, which released a shock of shoulder-length silver hair. "Well, detective investigator, what can I do for you?" she asked, looking at the two of them suspiciously, as if they were conspiring against her.

"Can I get you a gin and tonic?" Paula asked Belle, in an effort to defuse the tension.

"Yes, please," Belle said. She sat on a stuffed chair between the two sofas, crossed her legs, folded her arms across her chest, and stared at Fernando.

"I was hired to find out who killed Danny Ortiz," Fernando said. "Hired by his wife."

Belle frowned. "Frankly I don't give a tinker's damn about Danny Ortiz. He was a leech, a parasite. He was always asking Dallas for money because he couldn't support himself. Dallas was too sympathetic. He should have cut Danny loose years ago."

Paula reappeared. "Here's your gin and tonic."

"Thank you," Belle said and sipped the drink.

Fernando tried again. "Danny's wife thinks Travis Walker might have something to do with Danny's murder. Walker and the men who work for him. So I went up to the ranch Walker's renting in Taos this morning and tried to talk to your husband, thinking he might know something about what happened. But I found him incoherent. Heavily drugged."

Fernando chose not to tell her about his run-in with Walker's men in the parking lot at the ranch.

"Of course he's incoherent!" Belle shot back. "He's a drug addict and an alcoholic! He's halfway to dementia if he's not already there! That's why I'm divorcing him!"

Fernando nodded and then asked, "Do you think your husband's being held against his will?"

Belle sighed. "Oh for God's sake, what difference does it make? He went up there on his own free will. I tried to warn him because I knew what would happen. Travis has always provided him with drugs. They go back a long way. Travis is a great manipulator. He's fleeced Dallas for years, first as the manager of his band and then as his drug connection."

They heard another golf cart pull up outside the casita.

Belle turned to look at the front door and then said quickly, "But not for much longer. My lawyer will have divorce papers filed by the end of the week. I'm getting out with my half now before Dallas pisses it all away."

Her face brightened when the front door opened and a darkly handsome young man walked in. He was dressed in hiking clothes and carried a backpack, which he tossed on the floor.

"Sorry we're late, Belle," the young man said. "We found a trail leading into the mountains on the hill behind the resort. I guess we got carried away."

Belle smiled, the first time Fernando had seen her smile.

"Where's the cold beer?" asked the young man's companion, who followed him through the door. Much older, he had the build of an NFL linebacker, with a bushy black beard tinted with gray. He also wore hiking clothes.

Paula laughed. "Coming."

Belle turned back to Fernando. "Mister Lopez, this is Scott, Dallas's manager. And over there with the big beard is Larry, our driver and stage hand."

"Nice to meet you," Fernando said.

Both men waved.

"So," Fernando said. "Are you all staying in this casita?"

"Yes," Belle said quickly. "The casita has four bedrooms and four baths. And it should for what I'm paying. This place costs more per night than the down payment on our first house in Austin!"

Everyone laughed.

Paula returned with three beers, one of which she handed to Fernando.

"Much obliged," was all he could think to say. He loved her smile.

10

On the way to his office next morning Fernando stopped at an auto glass shop on Cerrillos Road and had the rear right window of his Cherokee replaced. Took longer to vacuum out the busted glass with a Shop-Vac than it did to replace the window. While waiting Fernando brooded about how to tell Oralia Ortiz that he had no leads, no hard information connecting anyone to the murder of her husband. Maybe it was time to turn the page and move on with her life and save herself some money. He hated to give up on any investigation, but his instincts told him this one would turn out to be hopelessly murky and maybe impossible to resolve with any degree of certainty.

When his cell phone rang he saw Hank Mathews' name appear on the screen. "Mornin' Hank," he said, picking up the phone.

"Howdy, Fernando," Hank said. "Listen, now I am interested..."

"Say what?"

"I am interested in that Painted Skull Ranch you mentioned earlier," Hank said. "We've had some developments up here and could use your help. Something's not right."

"Yeah?"

"We found a body on Highway Sixty-four just outside our city limits," Hank explained. "Whoever dropped off the body just tossed it in the damned ditch and drove off. Young man, looks to be in his mid thirties, no I.D. He was wearing one of those nylon outfits that bicycle riders wear. Forensics tells me he died of an overdose with enough fentanyl in his bloodstream to kill an elephant. I'm wondering if he's one of the people you saw at Painted Skull Ranch."

"Sounds like a kid I saw up there. He had a bag of fentanyl pills on his night table."

"Also, we did a little research on that ranch. Like I told you before, Bill Candelaria owns the ranch now. He's the only surviving member of the Candelaria family as far as anyone can tell. Well, it turns out old Bill hasn't been seen in going on two months. No one up in Pueblo knows what the hell happened to him. Seems a neighbor called the police and reported Bill missing. The police forced the lock and found his condo deserted. Looked like the place hadn't been used in weeks. So now we got ourselves a missing person and a dead person up here in Taos and maybe the two are connected."

Fernando didn't know what to say. The investigation—if he could call it that—kept getting more complicated.

"Hell, we don't even know if this Travis Walker guy has been renting the ranch or just squatting there."

"Okay," Fernando said, checking his watch. "I can be in Taos by one o'clock. Is that too late?"

"No. Let's meet at the morgue in Holy Cross Hospital. Holy Cross is on the south side of town, off Paseo del Cañon East."

"Hard to refuse an invitation to meet at the morgue," Fernando said. "That's the second one so far this week. I must be popular."

Hank laughed and clicked off.

Fernando decided to skip lunch and leave for Taos right away. He could eat later. He didn't bother going home for his overnight bag because he planned to be back in Santa Fe come nightfall. Instead, he hit the road as soon as his Cherokee was ready. He followed the highway north to Pojoaque where he had a fleeting urge to take the scenic high road to Taos through the mountains, but then decided to take the faster low road along the Rio Grande. He was fortunate that Holy Cross was on the south side of Taos, well before the logjam of tourists slowed traffic to a snail's pace. So just over an hour later he turned right on Paseo del Cañon East and cruised into the hospital parking lot on Weimer Road.

He saw Hank's cruiser parked across the way. Hank was just getting out of the vehicle. Slowly, because of his arthritic knees.

Fernando waved and walked over to join the big lawman with the black Stetson cocked back on his head.

"You must have driven like a bat out of hell," Hank said, pulling his Stetson lower on his forehead.

"No traffic until I hit Ranchos de Taos."

"Damn tourists," Hank muttered.

Fernando followed Hank into the hospital and down the elevator to the basement. They walked along the tile corridor to the end, where the morgue blocked their way. Hank rang and waited for the doors to open. Then the two of them stepped inside the frigid room. Hank removed his Stetson and pressed it to his chest as though he were about to pray.

"Howdy, Hank," the pathologist greeted them. He was a tiny man wearing a mask and goggles, looked like some kind of alien or mad scientist.

"Ray, this is Fernando," Hank said. "He's helping me with the investigation."

"Nice to meet you," Ray said.

Fernando waved.

Ray led them to a wall of drawers in back and pulled open one of the drawers.

Fernando immediately recognized the body in the drawer. He raised his hand. "That's him. That's the young guy I saw at the ranch. He didn't look much better back there."

Both Hank and the pathologist glanced at Fernando.

"Okay, thanks doc," Hank said. "That's all we needed to know."

Fernando followed Hank back outside to the parking lot. "So what now? What's your plan?"

Hank sighed. "Well, shit...I guess we better pay a visit to Mister Travis Walker and his guest ranch. We don't have a search warrant, so we'll have to play nice, pretend it's just a friendly visit. See what we can find out."

Fernando laughed. "They're not exactly a friendly bunch."

"If we don't like what we see, we'll work on a search warrant later," Hank said. "Then we won't have to act nice!"

Hank stopped before getting into his cruiser. "Wanna ride with me? I can bring you back here afterwards."

"Sure," Fernando said and climbed into the cruiser.

Hank avoided the congested Plaza area by following Paseo del Cañon as it skirted the southeastern side of the city and connected with Highway 64 East. He turned right on Highway 64 and hit the brake when he saw the totem pole on the left side of the road. "Is that the drive? I haven't been out here since old Bill lived at the ranch. Must be a good five years."

"That's it," Fernando said. "It's a ways in, just beyond the fence."

Hank pulled into the drive and stopped the cruiser. "What the hell? Is that a real human skull?"

"Sure looks like it," Fernando said. "Same thing I wondered when I saw it the first time."

"I expected to see a wood carving. What kind of fool would paint a real human skull's eyes red?"

Fernando shrugged.

"Well, it better not be Native American or somebody's gonna be in big trouble! Damn newcomers don't know what they're doing," Hank said and hit the accelerator.

The big cruiser splattered gravel as it pulled into the parking lot next to the Cadillac Fernando had seen on his last visit. The gray Audi was not in the lot. Neither were Travis Walker and his hired hands. Fernando held back and allowed Hank to lead the way.

"Yeah...this place looks a lot like the Martinez Hacienda," Hank said. "I remember it now."

Walking down the hill from the parking lot Fernando spotted Jerry, the tall gangly man who worked for Travis Walker as a caretaker. With his stringy red hair, Jerry looked like a scarecrow. His torn jeans and faded flannel shirt added to the scarecrow look.

At the moment Jerry was on his knees laying new flagstone on the walkway to the house. He looked up at them and grimaced. He had a black eye and a bandage over his nose.

"What happened to you?" Fernando asked.

Jerry looked away. "Mister Walker got upset."

"Upset about what?"

Jerry shrugged.

"Where is Mister Walker?" Hank asked.

Jerry pointed to the house.

Hank walked to the house and opened the front door, inviting himself in. "Hallooo! Anybody home?"

Fernando followed Hank inside.

Travis came out of his office and hurried into the kitchen. He stopped when he saw the big man with the badge and the Stetson hat. "Can I help you?"

"I sure hope so, son," Hank said. "I sure do."

Travis glanced from Hank to Fernando and frowned, a hint of concern flashing across his face.

"So I hear you're running a guest ranch here, is that right?" Hank asked. "I'm interested."

Travis nodded. "Yes, we operate a rustic guest ranch, lots of quiet rest and relaxation," he said, starting up his sales pitch. "You won't find a swimming pool or a golf course or anything like that here. Our guests meditate and go for long walks in the mountains. Sometimes we have live music performed by some of our musical guests. Otherwise we leave our guests alone. They can do anything they want—or nothing at all. We offer a breakfast buffet, boxed lunches, and catered dinners. We also sell recreational marijuana now that it's legal in New Mexico. I think you'd find it quite relaxing if you, or someone you know, is interested."

"Un-huh, sounds nice," Hank said. "So you're renting the place from old Bill Candelaria then?"

Travis took a second to respond. "That's right."

"So then you wouldn't mind if I just took a quick look at the papers, would you? Just so I could put my mind at ease. You know, see that you're certified and legal and such."

"Well...the thing is, I don't have the papers here," Travis said. "Anyway, it was more of a gentleman's agreement. A shake of hands."

"Well now, you don't say?" Hank removed his Stetson and brushed back his salt and pepper hair. "Thing is, this property has been in the Candelaria family for near two hundred years. I doubt old Bill would let some stranger rent it on a handshake. You see my problem."

Fernando watched Travis closely. Hank intimidated most people, but Travis just stood there looking at them with the same cold, hard stare. He didn't flinch; he didn't bat an eye.

"Course, I maybe could see someone as slick and well-spoken and handsome as you bamboozlin' old Bill to get control of his family's historic ranch, if that's what happened," Hank drawled in his best down-home voice. "Is that what happened? Did you bamboozle old Bill?"

Travis shook his head. "Just ask Bill if you don't believe me."

"See, that's just the thing. Old Bill seems to have disappeared. You wouldn't happen to know anything about that, would you?"

Travis laughed.

"Say, how about you show us around the ranch. Can you do that?"

After a long pause Travis said, "Okay. Why not? Follow me."

They followed Travis into the hallway past his office, its open door revealing a desk and bookshelves on one side of the room and a single bed and trastero on the other. Then they walked on by the row of tiny bedrooms, all of them empty at the moment. The closer they came to the back room the more they smelled the acrid scent of marijuana. The smell was coming from the patio outside, where several of the ranch's guests were gathered smoking weed.

Dallas and Jenny sat on the bench. Or rather Dallas sat on the bench and Jenny sat in his lap with her arm wrapped around his neck. They sucked on a number and then passed it to a middle-aged man sitting next to them on the cane-backed rocking chair. The man in the rocking chair wore a Colorado Rockies baseball cap and an olive green work shirt bearing a logo that read 'Al's Heating'. On another bench across the way two younger men mooned over each other and shared a number.

The guests paused their smoking to stare at Hank when he stepped outside onto the patio.

"Damn!' Hank said, swatting at the clouds of smoke. "You don't even have to light up to get high out here, all you have to do is walk through the smoke."

Everyone laughed. Sort of.

Travis pointed to the bungalows on the other side of the courtyard. "Those are casitas for long-term guests. Some of our guests stay a week or more. The bedrooms inside are for one or two nights."

Hank noticed the morada and clicked his tongue. He pointed at the morada. "Is that what I think it is?"

"The morada? Yes, it's part of the original property," Travis said. "The ranch had its own Penitente *cofradia.*"

"Is that where you got the skull in the driveway?" Hank asked. "From the morada graveyard?"

"Well, some of the bones from the cemetery washed up in the arroyo behind the morada," Travis said. "It seems appropriate to use it as a kind of *memento mori,* don't you think?"

Hank didn't respond.

Travis resumed his sales pitch. "You know, in some ways we're similar to the Penitentes. We just offer a different kind of self-therapy than the Brotherhood. We don't believe in penance through physical suffering. In fact, we don't believe in absolution at all, given the fact that we are all born naturally weak and selfish and what some might call sinful. We offer something much better, something that remedies the pain and suffering of human life. We offer the peace and forgetting that comes with Nirvana. Freud called it the death wish, but it's really the desire to escape pain and suffering."

Ignoring the con man's sales pitch, Fernando sidled up to Dallas. "Do you want to get out of here? You can leave with us," he whispered.

Dallas looked up with tired eyes and a deeply wrinkled forehead, a woebegone look on his face. "Nooo, I can't leave now. No way. My wife's trying to kill me, buddy."

"What do you mean?" Fernando asked.

Dallas ignored him.

Jenny tightened her grip around Dallas' neck. "Come here, baby, Jenny'll protect you jes like I always do."

Fernando gave up when the old cowboy musician began noodling Jenny's ample breasts.

He'd also heard enough of Travis' bullshit. He stepped forward and raised his voice: "You don't offer anything here but drugs!"

Travis spun around to face Fernando. "What better way to—"

Hank raised his hand and cut him off. "Okay, let's cut to the chase, Walker. Here's the thing. The young man whose body was found on the highway hereabouts was one of your guests. We know that because my friend Fernando here saw him in one of your bedrooms. The kid died from an overdose of fentanyl. Marijuana might be legal in New Mexico these days, but fentanyl for damned sure ain't. You understand what I'm saying?"

Just then the two men who had threatened Fernando in the parking lot came walking up to the patio. They had been waiting behind the house. The big man had his fists balled.

Travis, spotting them, shook his head and motioned with a subtle movement of his hand for them to stand back, which they did. They glared at Hank. Hank glared back at them.

Fernando stepped forward. "I found a plastic bag filled with blue pills on the kid's bedside table. You were providing him with illegal fentanyl from Mexico."

"No!" Travis snapped. "Our guests bring their own drugs. We have a strict don't ask, don't tell policy. The only medicinal drug we sell is marijuana. They stay as long as they want; they leave whenever they want. We don't control them."

Hank was about to say something but Travis continued. "So unless you have a search warrant, get off my property. Leave!" He pointed to the parking lot.

Hank scowled. Then he turned and walked away without saying a word or looking at the two thugs who stood back and made way for him. The big man's fists were still balled, just in case.

Fernando followed Hank off the patio and up the flagstone walkway to the parking lot. Jerry, the caretaker, waved as they walked by and asked, "Is Mister Walker still upset?"

"I'd keep your distance," Fernando said. "He's liable to be upset for a good long while."

Fernando decided not to tell Hank about his brief conversation with Dallas. Not yet anyway.

They climbed into the cruiser and sat there for a few moments watching Jerry at the bottom of the hill. Soon the two gorillas joined Jerry and stood there staring at them from a safe distance.

"Those boys could be trouble," Hank said, driving off. "Especially the big ugly one. Travis I'm not worried about."

1 1

By the time Fernando pulled into the parking lot in front of his office on Canyon Road the day was pretty much shot. Five o'clock and the sun had already disappeared behind the tall cottonwoods on East Alameda Street. The trip to Taos had left him with a sour taste in his mouth, which just contributed to his overall bad attitude. He didn't trust any of them, Dallas, Travis, Jenny, or anyone else he'd encountered at the ranch, especially the two tough guys who worked for Travis. Hank was right: they could be trouble.

He didn't know what to make of Dallas now. This time Dallas seemed more coherent. Then again, he'd accused his wife of trying to kill him. Belle had airs, no doubt about it, but a murderer?

Grumbling to himself, he climbed out of the Cherokee and walked into his office. He could hear Ruby talking to someone up in her gallery, which meant she had her windows open. He went directly to his mini-refrigerator and grabbed a Modelo. He popped open the can and took a long drink. The cold beer perked him up and so he took another long drink. Feeling better, he sat down at his desk and found a message on his desk phone.

"Uh...Mister Lopez?" said a vaguely familiar voice. "This is Paula at Bishop's Lodge Resort, Belle Longstreet's assistant? I'm calling to ask if we could meet later today...I found something that might be important. I'm meeting a friend in town for dinner at seven tonight. I could stop by your office around six o'clock. Would you be available?"

Something important? He had no idea what she meant, but he did enjoy her friendly voice.

So Fernando dialed the number she left on his machine and listened to the phone ring several times. He was about to give up when Paula answered. "I can't talk now," she whispered.

"Okay, six at my office is fine," he blurted out as fast as he could.

"Thank you," she said.

Fernando took that as a confirmation. While he waited he helped himself to another can of Modelo. About six o'clock he heard a car pull into the parking lot out front. He walked over to the window and looked out at a blue Honda Accord with Texas license plates. When the driver's door opened, he saw Paula step out of the Accord and then reach back into the car for her purse. Then she walked spritely across the gravel parking lot to his office. He held the door open for her.

Paula wore a low-cut red dress with a silver necklace and a sandcast silver bracelet. A knockout.

Fernando couldn't help himself. "Wow! You look great."

Paula blushed. "Dinner with an old friend. At the Compound."

"Lucky guy," he said.

"Why, Mister Lopez, you're an old flirt," Paula responded.

"Hah! Old is the operative word there, I'm afraid."

Fernando offered her a chair and sat at his desk. "So what did you find that might be important?"

"Well, here, let me show you," she said, taking an envelope out of her purse and holding it open over his desk. Torn pieces of a personal check fluttered out of the envelope and scattered on his desktop.

He looked at her for an explanation.

"It's a check signed by Dallas to Danny Ortiz for one thousand dollars," Paula said. "I found the torn check in the waste basket in Larry's room at our casita. Larry, you might remember, is Dallas and Belle's driver and stage hand. I drove up from Austin on my own because I plan to stay on another week or so with an old boyfriend. If it works out."

"Your dinner date," Fernando interjected.

"Yes," she said.

"So what's the significance of this torn check?"

"Well, the check is dated last Friday, the day Dallas left for Taos and the day before Danny was killed. Maybe Danny never received the check, but if he did..." She glanced at him. "You see?"

Fernando nodded. "If Danny did get the check, then Larry or somebody else took it from him—maybe from his dead body. If Danny never received the check, then how did Larry get his hands on it?"

"Exactly," she said. "And I don't think Larry would dare take a check from Dallas, so I'm guessing he took it from Danny."

"Unless, of course, Dallas decided not to give the check to Danny and instead tore it up and dropped it in Larry's waste basket," Fernando said.

Paula shook her head. "I don't think so. Dallas never went into our bedrooms—never. And he spent very little time at the casita anyway."

"Sounds like you might be right," he said. "What can you tell me about this Larry fellow? The driver."

Paula sighed. "He's kind of a rough character, but he's very loyal. Especially to Belle. He's been with them for many years, a lot longer than I have. Like the rest of us, he takes his orders from Belle. Dallas is...well, let's just say, more distant."

"You mean stoned?" Fernando asked.

"Yeah, sometimes," she said. "Back home he's usually off playing music with his friends or carousing the bars and honkytonks down on Sixth Street. If you've been to Austin you know about Austin's entertainment district. One big party all the time. We rarely see him at home. The same here."

"Back to Larry," Fernando said. "Have you ever seen him violent?"

Paula shook her head. "Not really. I've seen him get into shouting matches with people. Oh, and once when a drunk crashed the stage at a concert in New Orleans Larry punched the guy in the mouth and kicked him off the stage. Other than that, I've never seen him get violent."

"What about the other member of your entourage? Dallas' manager?"

"Scott?" Paula asked. "He's new. Belle brought him on board when Dallas downsized his band and started giving acoustic concerts instead. Belle thought Dallas would make more money playing on his own, not having to pay for a band. But Scott is harmless. He's a puppy dog."

Fernando paused a moment, reflecting on all he'd heard. Finally he said, "Okay, here's the reason I ask about Larry being violent. I had a short conversation with Dallas up at the ranch today. I went back with the county sheriff and paid them another visit. Anyway, Dallas told me his wife was trying to kill him. Do you know anything about that?"

"Kill him? Belle?" Paula seemed shocked by the question. "Belle can be a little authoritarian, as you saw the other day, but I can't imagine her killing or conspiring to kill anyone."

"Why not?" Fernando asked. "She's divorcing Dallas. You heard what she said about him. Obviously there's no love lost between the two of them. Plus, he's giving away their money. He's a wastrel."

Paula looked dubious. "Yes, but I still can't imagine. Belle is a blueblood from the Virginia Tidewater. Believe me, she thinks very highly of herself." She laughed. "Very highly!"

Fernando nodded, not about to argue with that. "Well, thanks for the tip. I'll try to speak with Larry. What's his routine like? Is he ever alone?"

"He and Scott swim laps in the Bishop's Lodge pool every morning at ten," she said. "In the afternoon they usually hike or go into Santa Fe. I don't know what they do in town—visit the museums, I suppose. Or shop. What else is there to do here?"

Paula glanced at her watch. "Anyway, I need to get going. I don't want to be late."

"To meet your old boyfriend?" Fernando asked.

She laughed. "Let's hope he's better than he was the first time."

12

Fernando arrived early at Bishop's Lodge Resort. He needed time to find the swimming pool on the resort's expansive grounds. Following the signs, he found the pool near the Reception Building. He parked in the front lot and walked over to the plaza area where he had a clear view of the pool and bathhouse, both deserted. Not a swimmer or lifeguard in sight. Time check: 9:45. So he sat on a bench and waited, hoping that none of the staff would come around and ask what the hell he was doing loitering on private property.

A few minutes after ten o'clock he saw two men walking down the path from the casita area on the northern rim of the property. He recognized Larry and Scott. They went into the bathhouse and reappeared a few minutes later wearing their swimming trunks. Muscular, bulked up Larry provided a perfect contrast to Scott, who in a bathing suit looked like the proverbial wimp. Contributing to his less than impressive build, Scott's skin color resembled the underbelly of a fish—the whitest white Fernando had ever seen.

Fernando watched them jump into the pool and splash each other until Larry grabbed Scott and held him underwater for several frantic seconds. After a few minutes of roughhousing they began to swim laps. They thrashed their way across the pool, rested for a few seconds, and then thrashed their way back across the pool. They did maybe ten awkward laps. Larry called it quits first. He said something to Scott that made the younger man laugh and then climbed out of the pool. Once on the deck Larry shook himself off like a big dog. While Scott floated on the surface of the pool, Larry plopped down in a lounger and placed a towel over his face.

Fernando seized the opportunity. He left the plaza area and walked directly to the chain-link fence behind Larry's chaise. "Hey, Larry. Looks like swimming's not your thing, eh?"

The big man yanked the towel off his face. "You got that right." He turned to face Fernando. "Who are you?"

"You don't remember me? I had a beer with you the other day. At the casita."

"Now I remember," Larry said. "You're the investigator. So what's up? Who you investigating today?"

"I wanted to ask you a question," Fernando said. "What do you know about a thousand-dollar check Dallas wrote to Danny Ortiz this past Friday, the day he left for Taos?"

Larry frowned. He seemed taken aback. "Nothing. Why would I?"

"Because the check was found in your room at the casita," Fernando said. "Torn into pieces and tossed in your waste basket."

Larry sighed. He stood and walked slowly to the fence. Then he grabbed the fence and glared at Fernando. "News to me."

"Then how do you explain its presence in your waste basket?"

"I don't have to explain anything to you."

Fernando raised his hand. "Here's the thing, Larry. The fact that you had the check in your possession means you took it from Danny either before or after he died. If you took it from Danny after he died, it means you were involved in his killing. You see your problem?"

Larry continued to glare at Fernando, hate in his eyes.

"Now I can take this check to my former colleagues at the Santa Fe Police Department. They'll do a DNA and fingerprint analysis, and if your DNA and fingerprints are on the check, as they will be, they'll come looking for you. Or, if you come clean with me now, I might forget all about the check. So what's it going to be, Larry?"

"No!" Larry shot back. He rattled the chain-link fence with both hands. "I didn't like you when you came to question Belle, and I don't like you now! So beat it before I call security!"

"Suit yourself, Larry. You're making a big mistake."

With that, Fernando turned and walked away. He didn't want to get in a physical confrontation with the big man. Better to give Larry time to consider his predicament.

When Fernando reached the parking lot he could still see Larry standing at the fence watching him. Larry hadn't moved.

On his way back to town Fernando considered his options. Few to none. Even if he took the torn check to Manny and convinced the SFPD to do an analysis, and even if they found Larry's fingerprints and DNA on the check, that wouldn't necessarily mean Larry had anything to do with Danny's killing. Larry could have found or been given the check by someone else. Or someone at the casita could have planted the check in Larry's room. Too many possibilities and not enough hard evidence. The torn check by itself would never convince the Chief to launch a full investigation.

So he found himself at a dead end, both here and in Taos. Something had to break soon or he would have to admit defeat and tell Oralia he couldn't find Danny's killers.

Once in town he followed the Paseo around to Alameda Street and found a parking place near Saint Francis Cathedral. He climbed out of the Cherokee and walked across the front steps of the historic basilica, past the statue of Archbishop Lamy and into Cathedral Park. He stopped in the shadows of the tall cottonwoods to get his bearings. If his information was correct, Danny had walked diagonally across the park, from the Cathedral at one end to Palace Avenue and the entrance to the Drury Hotel at the other. Yellow tape still roped off the area where Danny's body had been found near Palace Avenue.

Fernando walked in a direct line to the yellow tape, looking in the grass as he went and finding nothing. He stopped at the tape and noticed the matted grass where the struggle had occurred. Danny's assailants could have waited anywhere in the shadows and then jumped him before he could reach the lights of Palace Avenue. Afterwards they could have disappeared quickly by running behind the Cathedral to the big parking lot or Alameda Street, wherever they'd parked. In the darkness it would have been a quick, easy escape.

For the hell of it he walked up to the Drury Hotel and looked around. He spotted a row of windows on the first floor of the hotel overlooking the park. Maybe someone at the front desk had been working around eleven o'clock Saturday night and heard the men arguing in the park. And maybe they'd decided to take a look outside to see what the ruckus was all about. He decided to give it a try.

Inside the big doors he found the front counter straight ahead and a smaller desk for the concierge off to the side, near the windows overlooking the park. A smallish man dressed in a jacket and tie stood at the concierge desk talking to an elderly couple. The man in the jacket handed the elderly couple a brochure and pointed down Palace Avenue, evidently giving them directions, maybe to the Palace of the Governors or the Georgia O'Keeffe Museum, both of which were in that general direction. After they left Fernando stepped up to the desk.

"Can I help you?" the concierge asked, a friendly man with a big smile.

"I hope so," Fernando said. "Did you or anyone else at the Drury hear anything in the park last Saturday night when Danny Ortiz was murdered?"

The concierge lost his smile. "Are you a cop?"

"No, I'm a private investigator," Fernando said. "I'm working for Danny's widow, trying to find out who killed him."

The concierge glanced around the hotel lobby. Then he turned to Fernando. "Not me, but the night concierge did. He didn't say anything to the cops because he didn't want to get involved. He said he saw two guys hiding in the trees out in the park. He saw them jump Danny just before he reached Palace Avenue. He said the two of them seemed to be working together. One of them distracted Danny while the other one grabbed him from behind and knocked him down. After Danny fell one of them choked him from behind. Then they went through Danny's wallet and took off running."

"Did it look like a random encounter, or were they laying for him?" Fernando asked.

The concierge glanced around the lobby again. "Not random. He said the two guys were waiting in the shadows for Danny."

Fernando nodded. "Did he get a look at their faces? Could he identify them if he saw them again."

"No," the concierge said, shaking his head. "He said he didn't recognize either of them. It was too dark."

Fernando took a card out of his shirt pocket and handed it to the concierge. "Here, give this to your friend. Tell him if he can remember anything else to please give me a call."

"Will do."

"Okay. Much obliged."

Fernando left the hotel and walked slowly back to his Cherokee. He couldn't help but wonder what might have come to light if the police had conducted a thorough investigation. The night concierge, under proper questioning, might have remembered more details about the two men who attacked Danny. Who knows? Nobody wanted to get involved—not the witnesses, not the police. And that made his job a lot more difficult.

13

After dinner Fernando liked to relax on his patio with a cup of tea. The cool night air always invigorated him. Tonight a full moon shone over the cottonwoods along the acequia creating deep shadows on Estelle's rose garden. Some evenings he would sit out here for hours reflecting on the day's events. Brooding would be more like it, since he'd reached the age where he brooded about absolutely everything. No matter how much he mulled over the Danny Ortiz case, he had no idea what to do next. Was it even a case? Maybe the Chief had been right to refuse to waste precious resources on a no-account junkie like Danny.

While he sipped his coffee, he heard the phone ring inside. Moments later Estelle appeared on the patio. "A young woman's asking for you on the land line. She sounds upset."

Expecting Oralia, angry that he hadn't found Danny's killers, he shuffled into the kitchen and picked up the phone. "Yes?"

"Mister Lopez," a voice sobbed. "Can you help me? I don't know who else to call..."

Fernando recognized the voice. "Paula? What's happened?"

"I'm in trouble! They fired me! They found out I gave you the torn check and...can you help me?"

"Calm down," Fernando said. "Where are you?"

"I'm at the Inn on the Alameda," she wailed. "I checked in here after they kicked me out. They slapped me and twisted my arm and threatened to kill me."

"Who slapped you?"

"Larry, the driver. And Scott."

"Are they with you now?" Fernando asked.

"No, but they're coming back. They want me to sign a non-disclosure agreement. I don't know what to do. I'm afraid they'll hurt me...or worse!"

"How soon will they be back?" he asked.

"Soon!" Paula said. "They're on their way to Bishop's Lodge to get the document. They should be back in twenty or thirty minutes. Sorry to bother you, I'm just really afraid."

He sighed. "Okay, I'm on my way. Don't let them in if they arrive before I do, understand?"

"I understand," she said. She told him her room number at the inn and thanked him.

Fernando didn't bother to tell Estelle, who was already in the master bedroom preparing for bed. Why disturb her? Instead he buckled on his holster, just in case he had no other option but to use his Smith & Wessen, which was highly unlikely. Afterwards he quietly opened the kitchen door and stepped outside. He walked to his Cherokee and opened the back hatch, where he kept the tools of his trade. He ignored the baseball bat and instead chose a small crowbar. The twenty-inch iron crowbar slipped nicely into a belt loop on his jeans and hung by its bent claw on one end. The crowbar had come in handy more than once.

He drove to the end of Acequia Madre and turned right on the Paseo. Two blocks down he turned right again on East Alameda Street and then left into the parking lot of the Inn on the Alameda. He pulled into the first open space he saw and quickly cut the engine and the lights. Climbing out of the Cherokee, he paused a moment to listen but heard nothing. No loud voices, nothing. Satisfied, he began to move silently through the shadows in the dark parking lot, hugging one vehicle after another as he made his way around back. He had no way of knowing if Larry and Scott had already arrived. That meant he had to be cautious.

Up ahead he came finally to a walkway leading to the interior of the complex. He shrank back when he spotted a sickly yellow light splashing on the adobe walls inside the entrance. The light came from a ceramic fixture with slits that cast bars of light across a snarl of vines growing on the walls. The vines, thick as a man's arms, appeared to be moving, undulating like snakes. When he realized what it was, he edged forward into the feeble light. The walkway took him to an interior courtyard as dimly lit as the entranceway.

Fernando stopped to let his eyes adjust to the darkness. The casitas on either side of the courtyard came into focus. Each of them had a small patio behind a waist-high adobe wall and a wooden gate. He shuffled slowly down a narrow sidewalk toward the last casita, the one closest to the Paseo. Coming closer he saw a small pile of piñon wood stacked beside the door of the casita. The room number matched the one Paula had given him. By this time he was convinced that Larry and Scott hadn't yet arrived. Otherwise he would have heard their angry voices and Paula screaming.

He opened the gate and walked up to Paula's door. Through the blinds he could see a faint light inside. He knocked softly on the door and stepped back. Moments later the blinds parted and Paula peeked out at him.

He heard the dry click of the locks and then the door opened. He saw the damage immediately. Her face was red and swollen, her eyes puffy. The neckline of her blouse had been ripped in front revealing the top of her bra.

Paula reached out and pulled him inside and then slammed the door closed. "Thank you for coming," she said, composing herself. "I'm really scared. They followed me here and threatened to kill me unless I kept quiet about the check."

"Does Belle know about this?" Fernando asked.

"Of course she knows," Paula said. "She fired me. She sent Larry and Scott after me. She's capable of anything, you have no idea."

"Okay then, get your stuff together," Fernando said. "Let's get you out of here before they return. I can take you to a Residence Inn or somewhere out of the way. But hurry!"

She followed his advice, stuffing everything she found lying on the bed and in the bathroom into her suitcase and zipping it closed. "I'm ready," she said finally, grabbing her purse from the bedside table.

Fernando lifted her suitcase and reached for the door when he heard Larry and Scott outside on the sidewalk.

"Shit!" he said out loud.

Paula shrank back from the door.

He turned to face her. "Let me handle this. You stay inside and lock the door behind me. Whatever happens, don't open the door. If you need to, call the front desk for help."

Fernando opened the door and stepped outside just as Larry reached the patio gate. Scott held back when he saw Fernando, looking embarrassed and uncomfortable. It came as no surprise that Larry would be the one he'd have to deal with now. The bigger they come, the harder they fall.

"Well, well, look who it is," Larry said, coming into the patio. "Mister private dick himself."

"Leave her alone," Fernando said flatly, without emotion. It was a statement, an order. He wasn't asking.

Larry smiled. "Sure, we'll leave her alone, just as soon as she gives us what we want. You got a problem with that?"

"Leave her alone," he said again, staring at Larry.

Larry moved forward. "Get out of my way!"

Scott turned away, trying to make himself invisible.

Larry pushed Fernando back against the door and kept coming closer, over confident.

Fernando waited until Larry swung a wild right hand. Ducking, Fernando grabbed the claw of his crow bar. Coming up with the crow bar in his right hand he swung the steel bar up over his head and brought it down as forcefully as he could on Larry's outstretched arm. He heard the bone in the forearm crack. For good measure he swung the crow bar around and hit Larry's arm again as he fell.

Larry screamed out in pain. He dropped to his knees, his right arm hanging limply from his shoulder. He reached over with his left hand and cradled the arm, moaning loudly.

Fernando turned to Scott, who now looked sick, as if he were about to vomit on the sidewalk. "You better get him to an emergency room fast," Fernando said. "That arm won't mend without surgery."

Scott nodded. He came over to Larry and tried to help the big man stand up, but Larry howled with pain when touched. It took some time, but Scott finally managed to get Larry on his feet and help him walk back to the sidewalk. Just before they disappeared through the walkway Larry turned and cursed at Fernando. "I'll kill you for this...I'll fucking kill you!"

Fernando saluted. He'd heard it all before.

He waited until he heard Scott and Larry's car drive off and then went back inside the casita. Paula was watching from the side window. "Thank you," she said. "I don't know what I would have done..."

He grabbed her suitcase. "Are you ready? You can follow me to the Residence Inn on Galisteo. They'll never find you there. Even if they try."

He waited on the interior patio while Paula went to the office and checked out. Then he followed her to the parking lot and loaded her suitcase in the back of her Honda Accord.

"Now, give me your phone," Fernando said.

She handed him her cell phone.

He turned it off and handed it back. "Don't turn it back on until you leave the Residence Inn. If you need to call me, use the room phone."

Paula nodded.

"Okay, follow me," Fernando said. He walked quickly to the other side of the parking lot and climbed into his Cherokee. With Paula following in her Honda, he turned left on the Paseo and then left again on Don Gaspar. At the top of the hill he turned right on Cordova and then left on Galisteo to the Residence Inn on the corner of Galisteo and Saint Michael's Drive.

Both of them stopped in front of the office. Fernando got out of the Cherokee and walked over to the Accord. "Do you want me to check in for you?"

"No, I'm much calmer now," she said. "I can do it."

When she came back with the keycard, he followed her around back to the appropriate number. He parked the Cherokee next to her Accord and then carried her suitcase up the wooden steps to a second-floor room.

Paula switched on the lights and walked into the spacious suite. "This will do just fine."

Fernando helped himself to a stuffed chair by the door and watched while she unpacked a few items from her suitcase. When finished she joined him, sitting on a small sofa facing a gas fireplace.

"So what did Belle say when she fired you, if you don't mind talking about it?" he asked.

"She accused me of being disloyal," Paula replied. "She said I'd betrayed them. I thought I was just doing the right thing, but I guess I was naïve. That's all she said before leaving. She was on her way to Taos and didn't bother to explain. She took one of the lender cars Bishop's Lodge provides for its guests. So I don't know for sure if she sent Larry and Scott after me, but it's logical. I mean, she's the boss. She gives the orders."

"Taos? Why was she going to Taos?"

"She's off to the Sagebrush Inn for one of her many trysts," she said. "Her 'dates,' as she calls them. She and Dallas both have tons of extramarital affairs. They've never been monogamous. I used to think it odd, but the more I see of married people, I wonder. Is anyone monogamous these days?"

Fernando shook his head. "Good question."

She laughed. "What about you? Are you monogamous, Mister Lopez?"

He shrugged and changed the subject. "So what will you do now?"

"I'll probably go back to Austin and try to get another job," Paula said. "If Belle tries to bother me in Austin, then I can always go stay with my parents in Miami Beach. They retired there a couple of years ago. I know I could find a job as an event planner at one of the hotels in Miami, there's so many of them. When I wasn't working I could lie on the beach and relax for a change. The last few months have been very stressful. Working with these people...well, it's been tough."

He laughed. "I can see that."

While they talked she left the sofa and climbed onto one of the queen-sized beds across the room.

Fernando stood up. "Well, I should be going."

"Could you just stay a little while longer?" Paula asked. "Please? Just keep me company for a while?"

"Okay."

He went to sit back down but Paula patted the bed beside her. "Can you sit next to me? I would feel so much better."

Fernando looked at her. "Maybe you should call your boyfriend."

"Hah!" she said. "He's useless. I called him tonight before I called you. You know what he said? 'Not my thing.'"

Fernando didn't know what to say so he said nothing.

"I mean, he's a nice enough guy, a little wishy-washy and self-absorbed, but useless in a crisis...and not prepared to deal with someone like Larry."

Fernando nodded.

"I have my doubts about it. I mean him," she said softly.

Fernando walked quietly to the bed and lay down next to Paula. She snuggled up to him and rested her head on his shoulder.

Feeling uncomfortable, he watched Paula cuddle. He couldn't help but notice how attractive she was, even with her bruised face. For a moment he was tempted to kiss her. If he were ten years younger he probably would have and then who knows what trouble he would have gotten himself into. Lotta complications, that's what. Thinking about it gave him a headache. As it was he just wanted to find a way to extricate himself as politely as possible.

Out of exhaustion he closed his eyes. Sometime later a siren on Saint Michaels Drive woke him. He had no idea how long he'd been asleep. He checked his watch: nearly two a.m.

Fernando gently lifted Paula's arm off his waist and slowly eased out of the bed. He checked to make sure he hadn't awakened her and then shuffled quietly to the front door.

One more look behind him and then he left, closing the door behind him and making sure it was locked.

He walked stealthily down the stairs to the parking lot. A full moon bathed the Cherokee in yellow light. Sneaking out of a woman's bed in the middle of the night made him feel like a damned lothario!

14

After breakfast Fernando grabbed his worst-scenario overnight bag and prepared to hit the road. He was on his way to Taos again, this time to the Sagebrush Inn. He wanted to see for himself just who Belle Longstreet was meeting at the Sagebrush. His instincts told him the identity of Belle's paramour might be the missing link that would make all the pieces of the puzzle fit together. Over the years he'd learned to pay attention to his instincts. They were usually right on the money.

Once again Estelle had already left for work at the Saint Francis Outreach Program, so he didn't have to explain his plans before leaving. If needed, he would call her later from Taos.

He stepped outside and locked their front door. When he turned to walk to the Cherokee his cell phone rang, so he sat on a wooden bench overlooking Estelle's rose garden and answered the phone.

"Mister Lopez? This is Mike Romero."

Fernando wracked his brain, trying to remember a Mike Romero. He came up empty.

"I'm the night concierge at the Drury Hotel," Romero added. My friend Ray gave me your card and said you might want to talk about the Danny Ortiz murder."

"Oh...yes, thanks for calling," Fernando said. "When can we meet?"

"I'm free now. My shift doesn't start until five o'clock."

"Okay. Where are you now?"

"I'm downtown at the French Pastry Shop. Just finished breakfast."

"How about I meet you in the Plaza," Fernando said. "I can be there in ten minutes, maybe less."

"Sounds good," Romero said. "I'll be on a bench. You can't miss me, I'm wearing a red windbreaker."

"I'm on my way."

Fernando tossed his overnight bag in the back of the Cherokee and drove down the Paseo and turned left on Alameda Street, where he always parked. He found a parking place near the Cathedral and walked down San Francisco Street into the Plaza. He spotted a red windbreaker on the far side of the Plaza, near the Palace of the Governors. He waved and followed the sidewalk across the Plaza to the bench where Mike Romero was sitting.

"Thanks again for calling," Fernando said and sat on the bench.

"No problem," Romero said, a dapper young man wearing a red Lacoste windbreaker and chinos. He looked to be in his early thirties, with short black hair and a clean-shaven face and high cheekbones. He looked at Fernando closely. "You sure you're not a cop? You look like one."

Fernando laughed. "I used to be a police detective, now I'm a private investigator. Oralia Ortiz hired me to find Danny's killer. The police think it was a random encounter with a couple of drunks or homeless people, but Oralia thinks Danny was set up and intentionally murdered."

Romero shook his head. "Not a random encounter. The two men were waiting in the shadows for at least half an hour. I heard them talking outside the windows, so I went over and took a look. They were just talking, so I didn't think much about it at the time. Then, later, I heard them arguing, so I went back to the window and took another look. This time they were kind of wrestling with each other and shouting."

"Pretending to argue, you mean?" Fernando asked.

Romero nodded. "Then when Danny walked up they stopped fighting and attacked him, first one and then the other. One of them hit Danny and knocked him down and the other one jumped on top and started choking him. I watched the whole thing. Danny fought back but there wasn't much he could do. They had him pinned on the ground, two against one. It wasn't long before Danny stopped fighting and lay still. A few minutes at most."

"What did the two attackers do then?" Fernando asked.

"I guess they robbed him," Romero said. "They went through his pockets and his wallet."

"His pockets?"

"Yeah, Danny's shirt and pants pockets," Romero said. "They threw something back on the grass. Must have been Danny's wallet."

"Did you see or hear anyone else in the park?"

"No, it's unusual to find anyone in Cathedral Park after dark. That's why I went to the window in the first place. Because it was so unusual to hear voices outside our windows."

"And you didn't recognize either of the two guys who attacked Danny?" Fernando asked.

Romero shook his head. "No, it was too dark. I could just see shadows, not faces."

Fernando considered. "So what happened next? Did these two guys run away through the dark alley between the hotel and the Cathedral? Toward the parking lot and Alameda Street?"

'No, that's the thing I wanted to tell you," Romero said. "They had a car waiting for them. It was parked on Palace, up by the Paseo. I could actually hear it running through the window."

"Are you sure? How do you know the car was waiting for them?" Fernando asked.

"Because I saw them running up to the car and heard the car doors slamming. As soon as they finished with Danny, they ran directly to the car. I didn't actually see the car, but I heard it pull out on the Paseo and take off fast."

"Going in which direction?"

Romero shook his head. "I couldn't tell. Could have turned left or right."

"So they had an escape car," Fernando said, mostly to himself.

"They did," Romero said, "which is why it had to be planned. No way it was a random encounter. It was definitely a hit."

"I'll be damned. There was a third person involved."

Romero checked his watch. "Well, I have some errands to do today before work, so I better be going. Hope this helps you find Danny's killers."

Fernando thanked Romero and watched him walk across the Plaza and disappear into the crowd of tourists on Palace Avenue.

Fernando sat on the bench by himself for several minutes thinking about what he'd just heard. Three people. So who was the third man—or woman?

15

By the time Fernando rounded the curve into Ranchos de Taos the sun had long since passed its noon zenith and disappeared behind a bank of dark rain clouds moving in from the northwest. It didn't rain often in the sunny Southwest, but when it did the arroyos could flood and all hell could break loose. He was running late this morning, thanks partly to his meeting with Mike Romero, which had further muddled his investigation, and partly to a series of mishaps and misunderstandings that were, as usual, his fault.

Yesterday Estelle had asked to borrow his Cherokee at ten o'clock this morning for work. Her outreach program needed the big vehicle to deliver boxes of food to needy families in Santa Fe. He'd said yes but then forgot all about it after Mike Romero called. By the time he finally remembered he was on Highway 285 near Tesuque, so he had to turn off the highway at the second Tesuque exit and drive all the way back to Santa Fe on Bishop's Lodge Road. Estelle had been waiting for over a half hour when he pulled into their driveway on Acequia Madre. Furious, she lectured him on his thoughtlessness and accused him of suffering from memory loss. All he could do was plead guilty and apologize. No doubt about it, he should have remembered. His bad. Then to make matters worse he couldn't find his set of keys to Estelle's Camry, his loaner for the day. He searched everywhere for the damn keys before finally finding them in a kitchen utility drawer.

Coming into Taos Fernando decided to stop first at Hank's office. He wanted to check on the status of a search warrant for Painted Skull Ranch. He fought the stop and go traffic all the way to the Taos County Sheriff's Office and pulled into the parking lot on Lovato Place. He found Hank in his office with his feet up on his desk yelling orders into a phone. "Well find out, goddamnit!" Hank said, and slammed his desk phone down on his desk.

"One of those days, eh?" Fernando said, walking into the office and taking a seat.

Hank grinned. "Aren't they all, anymore?"

"Pretty much," Fernando said.

Hank raised his hand. "Don't even ask about the search warrant. The damn judge wants more hard evidence, so that's on hold until I can get a handle on this latest shooting out in Questa. Turns out a couple of small ranchers out there got in an argument about whose cattle can legally graze on a stretch of BLM land. Old Jack Ryan, who I've known for years, took matters into his own hands and started shooting Eloy Lucero's cattle. So then Old Eloy, who I've also known for years, took matters into his own hands and shot Jack dead."

"Which one had the grazing rights?" Fernando asked.

"That's what I'm trying to find out," Hank said. "I'm not sure either one of the yahoos had grazing rights up there. Eloy's a stubborn sonofabitch and so was Jack. Neither would back down."

"Those BLM leases are nothing but trouble," Fernando added.

"Tell me about it! So what brings you back to the wild West?"

Fernando explained what had happened at Bishop's Lodge and why he'd come to Taos. "I got a tip that Belle Longstreet is meeting someone at the Sagebrush for a romantic tryst. I want to know who that someone is. I have my suspicions."

"Yeah? Well, I don't know what the hell you expect to find, but good luck," Hank said, standing up and grabbing his Stetson on the coat rack behind his desk. "I'm on my way to Questa now."

"You too. Good luck in Questa," Fernando said.

"I hate that fucking place," Hank growled.

With that Fernando made his way outside. He looked unsuccessfully for his Cherokee until he remembered he was driving Estelle's Camry. Which was parked right in front of him.

Once in the Camry he drove directly to the Sagebrush Inn, a sprawling collection of interconnected adobe and faux adobe buildings. The original building dated from 1929, with the ends of its roof vigas protruding from the tan stucco. He pulled into the front lot and parked the Camry off to the side of the entrance. He walked under the portico and into the funky lobby, where thick vigas were exposed on the ceiling. The lobby was chock-full of antiques, from the handcrafted furniture and wrought iron light fixtures to the shelves of old bottles on either side of the tri-doors in front. Above the doors hung old portraits painted by local artists of Native Americans and famous Taoseños. Old Taos, everything about the place.

Fernando walked up to the front counter. A young man behind the counter smiled and said, "Can I help you?"

"Yeah, I'm here to meet Belle Longstreet," Fernando said. "Could you see if she's in her room?"

"Sure, let me check," the desk clerk said, a young man wearing a leather vest over a white shirt. He turned to his computer and hit a few keys and then scrolled down and then hit a few more keys. He shook his head. "I'm sorry, we don't show anyone by that name."

"Hmmm...I guess she hasn't checked in yet," Fernando said. "I'll stop back later."

Fernando walked outside and sat on a wooden bench under the portico. Either Belle wasn't at the Sagebrush or she'd registered using an assumed name. He suspected the latter.

He checked his watch and considered his options. Already three o'clock, which meant the cocktail hour was only two hours away. He decided to wait.

He went back inside and bought the day's Taos and Albuquerque newspapers and carried them into the Cantina, an old dimly lit bar with exposed vigas and varnished wooden logs holding up the ceiling. He found a corner table in the rear near an open fireplace. The clunky wooden chair and thick round table were uncomfortable, but at least he would be nearly invisible in the darkest part of the bar and yet still able to see the hallway leading from the front lobby to the Cantina and Dining Hall. If Belle walked by, he would see her.

Fernando spread out his newspapers and started reading. When a server came over he ordered his usual Modelo and sipped on it slowly over the next hour or so. About 4:30 he noticed the server giving him the Evil Eye. He was about to order another Modelo when he saw the two of them, Belle Longstreet and Travis Walker. They came strolling down the hall into the Cantina and sat across from each other at a table in the front of the cantina near a bank of windows. On the wall behind them hung an elk's head with massive antlers. Belle looked striking, resembling a Flamingo dancer with black tights and jacket over a flaming red blouse. Travis was more relaxed with jeans and a white shirt and silver bolo tie. They looked cozy together, too cozy.

Fernando waited while they ordered. As soon as the server brought them cocktails, he tossed his newspapers aside and walked directly to their table. Slowly, for maximum effect.

Belle's mouth dropped open when she saw Fernando. Travis actually jumped in his seat. For a moment Fernando thought Travis was going to get up and charge him. He didn't.

Fernando grabbed a chair and dragged it across the floor to their table, making as much noise as possible. Then he sat in the chair staring at them. "Aren't you two cozy," he said, not bothering to hide his sarcasm.

"What are you doing here?" Travis managed to say, sitting back down.

Belle refused to look at him, imperious as ever.

"I'm glad you asked," Fernando said. "I'm trying to find out which one of you killed Danny Ortiz."

Now Belle turned to face him. "Oh please, why would I kill Danny?" she snapped. "Me!"

"Because you wanted to stop him from taking money from Dallas," Fernando said. "You wouldn't do the deed yourself, of course. You sent your man Larry, isn't that right?"

"NO!" she screamed. She shot up from the table spilling her drink and then stomped out of the Cantina scowling. Travis watched her walk away with a look of abandonment on his face.

The spilled green liquor from Belle's drink drip, dripped onto the floor while Fernando waved goodbye.

Fernando turned suddenly to Travis. "Or maybe you sent your two goons to kill Danny. You wanted to stop him from taking Dallas away. You were worried he would persuade Dallas to leave your ranch, right?"

Travis shook his head angrily. Taking a moment to control his anger, he said, "No. My staff kicked him off the ranch because he was bothering our guests. They didn't touch him. That's not how we do business."

"What business is that? Selling drugs?"

Travis sighed. "I told you back at the ranch that we offer a rustic getaway. Rest and relaxation and forgetting. An escape from pain and suffering. The only drugs we sell are perfectly legal in the State of New Mexico. You know this, so what's your problem?"

Fernando smiled. "Oh come on, Danny was trying to get Dallas to leave the ranch. You wanted Dallas to stay so you could keep him addicted and sell him more drugs."

"Really? Do you really think I had that much power over Dallas Longstreet? Do you know who Dallas is?"

"He's an addict! Of course you have that much power over him!"

Travis glanced around, his hands shaking on the table. "Look...you don't know who you're dealing with here. You're in way over your head." With that he dropped a twenty-dollar bill on the table and walked out of the Cantina.

"I'll be in touch," Fernando shouted after him.

16

Fernando rolled up his newspapers and tossed them in the trash on his way out of the Sagebrush Inn. He drove the Camry into town and turned right on Kit Carson Road, following it past the Mabel Dodge Luhan House to where it became Highway 64. When he approached Painted Skull Ranch he slowed down and looked for a place to pull over. Just across the highway from the skull on the totem pole he noticed a vacant lot. He turned into the lot and parked behind a bank of chamisa. He could still see the highway, but a vehicle coming out of the ranch's driveway wouldn't be able to see the Camry. Then he waited. Waiting seemed to be the theme of the day.

Less than fifteen minutes later the old Ford pickup Fernando had seen in the parking lot of Painted Skull Ranch appeared in the driveway. The pickup bounced its way to the gate and then turned left on Highway 64 heading toward Cimarron. As he hoped, Jerry was driving the beat-up pickup, a splotchy blue Ford with rusted fenders. The truck misfired and belched black smoke when it stopped or accelerated.

Fernando eased the Camry onto the highway and followed at a safe distance, trying not to breath the toxic fumes spewing out of the pickup. The two vehicles wound their way through a series of canyons heading east into the foothills. Leaving the mountains they entered an expansive sagebrush prairie with isolated ranch houses scattered across the mostly open range, with an occasional barbed wire fence separating the ranches. Up ahead the Ford pickup signaled and then turned left onto a narrow dirt road that looked like it hadn't been maintained in years. The road curved around to a dilapidated house set back a good one hundred yards from the highway.

Fernando turned onto the dirt road and stopped. From his vantage point he could see what had once been an impressive two-story house with gables and a wrap-around porch. Now, gray and unpainted and sagging in the middle, the house looked like it was gradually collapsing from its own weight. The unsightly structure sat on a small patch of bare dirt, surrounded by a barbed wire fence that separated it from the greener prairie. The house looked abandoned, uninhabitable.

Fernando watched as the Ford pickup stopped in front of the house with one last belch of black smoke. Jerry climbed out of the cab and brushed himself off. Did the young man live there?

Not waiting, Fernando proceeded down the rough dirt road, the Camry bouncing over rocks and swerving to avoid ruts. He pulled in behind the Ford pickup and set his brake.

Jerry stared at him from the rickety porch. His black eye was an ugly purple now, ringed by his stringy red hair. He looked confused, not knowing what to do or say.

Fernando stepped out of the Camry and approached the porch. "Jerry, sorry to bother you. I saw you drive out of the ranch and thought I might trouble you for some information."

Jerry looked at him suspiciously. "I don't know if I should talk to you. Mister Walker warned me."

"Did Travis Walker's men beat you up?" Fernando asked. "Is that why you have a black eye?"

Jerry nodded. "So?"

"Why did they beat you?" Fernando asked. "Did it have anything to do with the young biker who died at the ranch? Did they attack you because of how you disposed of the biker's body?"

When Jerry didn't reply, Fernando asked, "They also beat up Danny Ortiz when Danny tried to get Dallas Longstreet to leave the ranch. Did you see them attack Danny?"

Jerry shrugged. "I wasn't there when it happened."

"Tell me the truth, Jerry. I know you're an honest man. Is Travis selling drugs at Painted Skull Ranch?"

Jerry glanced around, as if looking for help. "Maybe. It ain't none of my business. I didn't do anything wrong."

Fernando nodded, trying his best to show that he was sympathetic. "I know you didn't, Jerry. I appreciate your honesty. Do you know for a fact that Travis is renting the ranch from Bill Candelaria?"

"I guess he is," Jerry said. "I saw Mister Candelaria at the ranch a coupla months ago, must have been. I can't remember exactly."

Just then the door to the house swung open and a man in a wheelchair rolled out. "What the hell's going on out here? Who are you talking to?" the man in the wheelchair bellowed.

Fernando stepped back, looking up at an old man with shoulder length white hair holding a shotgun in his lap. He wore overalls over a white T-shirt. His wrinkled face was as pale as death.

"Goddamnit to hell! Who is that?" the old man shouted at Jerry and raised his shotgun.

"It's okay, daddy," Jerry said, grabbing the shotgun and lowering the barrel. "I know him from the ranch. From work."

The old man stared at Fernando, not convinced. "What the hell does he want? Why's he here?"

Jerry turned to Fernando. "This is my dad, Clyde. He don't mean no harm. We used to own over one thousand acres in this valley, but then my dad fell off his horse tending cattle and broke his back. We had to sell most of the ranch to pay his medical bills. This is all we have left now. He's kind of paranoid that people want to take more of his land. What little is left."

"Sorry to hear that," Fernando said.

"Run him off, goddamnit, or I will," the old man said, rocking his wheel chair back and forth on the porch.

Jerry turned to Clyde. "Put your gun away, daddy."

"Like hell I will!" the old man snapped.

Then Jerry tried to pull the shotgun out of Clyde's hands, but the old man fought back. The two of them struggled over the shotgun. Finally Jerry managed to wrestle it away from his father and push the wheelchair back.

Fernando raised his hands. Enough. Time to get the hell out of here before someone got hurt. "Okay, sorry to bother you folks. I'll be going then."

Jerry and his father watched him walk to the Camry and climb inside.

Fernando slammed the door and waved goodbye. He fired the engine and made a quick U turn, taking off fast. He didn't slow down until he hit the first bump. In the rear view mirror he saw a ribbon of dust spewing behind him.

Fernando came to a stop when he reached the highway. He sat there for a moment letting the engine idle. He'd hoped to have more time with Jerry to ask about the drugs, but suddenly he had a better idea.

17

Fernando switched on his headlights as he turned right onto Highway 64. The sun had long since disappeared behind the Taos Mountains to the west. The mountains crouched on the road ahead like huge beasts blocking his way, shadows deepening into shadows. Behind him a full moon hung in the eastern sky, bathing the sagebrush on either side of the highway in a soft yellow glow. He took his time, not fond of driving at night. Too many drunks and crazy people on the roads after dark. Anything could happen. To anyone.

When he entered the dark foothills Fernando slowed down even more. Soon he ran afoul of a speedster in a Mustang who raced up behind him and honked his displeasure. Impatient, the speedster raced around him and gave him the finger. Fortunately the Camry's bright lights reflected off the totem pole far enough in advance to give him time to spot the vacant lot where he'd parked earlier. He pulled off the highway into the dirt lot and again parked behind the chamisa bushes. He waited for a good fifteen or twenty minutes, watching the driveway across the road. No vehicles came in or out of the ranch. He expected Travis to be preoccupied with Belle back at the Sagebrush Inn. What better time to pay an unexpected call on Dallas? To give him one more opportunity to escape.

Satisfied, Fernando stepped out of the Cherokee. He decided to leave his Smith & Wessen in the glove compartment. The cool night air felt exhilarating. The moon had gone behind a bank of thin clouds, leaving him just enough light to see where he was going. He crossed the highway quickly and entered a ghostly landscape of juniper and piñon trees, their gnarled, twisted branches forming grotesque shapes in the darkness. He could smell the pine in the alpine air as he trudged over the rough terrain, avoiding the road. Just as the ocotillo fence came into view he heard the howl of a lone coyote off in the distance. All the night creatures were out hunting tonight.

When he reached the fence he walked back to the road and through the gate. From the small rise where he stood he could see the parking lot and Painted Skull Ranch below. Several windows were illuminated in the main house and in a couple of the bungalows. He avoided the house, circling to his left through the sage and saltbush on the hill. Soon he came to an arroyo, which he followed around behind the collapsed adobe buildings that had once been blacksmith and carpenter shops. The flat roofs had long since imploded and the walls partially collapsed, leaving jagged shapes in the moonlight.

The first bungalow was dark, so he crept quietly over to the second and peered into its curtain-less rear window. Inside a middle-aged man in a khaki work shirt lay face down on a single bed. Plastic bags and bottles of pills lay on the nightstand, along with a pipe. Fernando couldn't be sure, but it might have been the guy in the 'Al's Heating' shirt he'd seen on the porch during his last visit. He moved on, heading for the well-lit bungalow at the end. All the others were dark. This was his last, best hope for finding Dallas.

His spirits lifted when he heard a guitar screech and that familiar deep baritone voice: "Stay all night...stay a little longer...dance all night... huh, what...wait...dang me, I can't remember what comes next, darlin'... ahhh shit, I sung that song since I was a baby in my momma's arms..."

Fernando hugged the back wall of the bungalow and edged over to the rear window. He heard Dallas clearly now:

"I'll tell you what, my uncle Lou used to play that one on his fiddle for us kids...and that was before I ever started playing the guitar...aunt Rose used to sing...she had a helluva voice, high as Emmylou Harris...even higher when she was drunk!"

"Whaaaaat?" came another voice, Jenny's. "You can't remember your Bob Wills, daddy? You sure you're from Texas?"

"Hell, I am Texas," Dallas intoned.

By the time Fernando reached the window and looked in both Dallas and Jenny had quieted down some. Inside he saw Jenny lying on the bed, naked as a jaybird, with a twisted white sheet wrapped around her middle. Across the room Dallas sat on an old kitchen chair in his white underwear. Spread out on the kitchen table were several syringes and packets of white powder, along with a tourniquet and a spoon and a cigarette lighter. Dallas seemed to be fidgeting at the table, trying to make a decision about what to do next. When he noticed Jenny in bed, he tried to stand up and then fell back down heavily.

"Whoa Nellie," Dallas said.

Fernando moved around to the front of the bungalow and knocked softly on the door. When no one answered he opened it himself and stepped into the dusty bungalow. The dingy one-room unit smelled stale and moldy with a hint of marijuana and urine. The smell nearly gagged him.

Dallas looked up at him. "Say...where'd you come from? I think I've seen you before. This here's a private party. Why're you here?"

The question took Fernando by surprise. Why was he here? He was hired to find Danny's killers, not to save Dallas from himself, or from Belle and Travis and whatever plot they were concocting. Somehow, somewhere along the line, his investigation had taken a wrong turn. He'd gotten more involved with Dallas than Danny. Was it too late to get out now?

"Get rid of him!" Jenny said from the bed. She sounded angry.

Her voice brought Fernando back to the moment. He had to finish this, whatever it took. He wasn't a quitter.

"Listen, I can get you out of here," Fernando said to Dallas. "Take you to a rehab facility where you'll be safe from your wife. She's divorcing you and trying to take your money. You need to get a lawyer fast. Do you understand what I'm saying?"

Dallas nodded. "Yeah buddy! My wife's tryin' to kill me, I know. Thing is, I had a lawyer...but the sonofabitch is sidin' with Belle. The only friend I got left is ole Jenny over there." He pointed to the bed, where Jenny was sitting up now, glaring at Fernando.

"Look, I know it's none of my business," Fernando said, "but you're in danger if you stay here. So why not leave now while you're still able to walk out. Hell, take Jenny with you. Just get out!"

"Yeah...well...I don't know 'bout that," Dallas said and then turned to Jenny. "Jenny, you wanna get outta here?"

"No! I'm trying to sleep if you assholes would be quiet!"

Dallas frowned and shook his head sadly. "You see? Jenny don't want to leave."

"Then leave her and come with me," Fernando said. "You're dealing with dangerous people. They killed Danny. They may try to kill you."

Suddenly Jenny jumped out of the bed, holding the sheet over her tits. "Don't listen to him, daddy! Nobody's gonna kill you. Stay here with me. Jenny'll protect you like always."

Dallas threw open his arms. "You see?"

"Yeah, I see," Fernando said. He'd known plenty of self-destructive people who were unable or unwilling to take care of themselves. Each and every one of them had come to a bad end.

Dallas would be no exception.

With that, Fernando quickly snatched as many packets of white powder as he could and stuffed them in his pockets.

"Hey, buddy!" Dallas shouted and tried to grab Fernando. He lost his balance and fell forward onto the table.

Jenny screamed.

Fernando ran outside, worried that Jenny's scream would alert the two tough guys who worked for Travis. He kept to the shadows, circling around behind the bungalow. Just as he did he caught a glimpse of a flickering light down by the morada. The light had a bluish tone, not the soft yellow of the moonlight. He froze as he watched the blue light morph into the shape of a vortex spinning into what looked like a human form. Then the light quickly disappeared through the door of the morada. Intrigued, he decided to check it out, but as soon as he moved out of the shadows he began to have second thoughts.

Feeling exposed, he moved past the last bungalow into the courtyard. He told himself he should turn around and head back to the Cherokee and get the hell out of here. Yet he continued.

The light beckoned him, drew him forward. It was as if the light wanted him to see something inside the morada?

Earlier he'd been offended to learn that a sacred morada had fallen into the hands of someone like Travis. For decades Anglos had maligned and sensationalized the Penitentes and their neighborhood moradas. True, some of the Brotherhoods had carried crosses and engaged in self-flagellation during Holy Week, but this was only one aspect of their work as lay religious organizations associated with the Catholic Church. What the critics didn't understand was that the Brothers played a central role in the communities where their moradas were located. They fed the impoverished, nursed the sick, and buried the dead. It pissed him off that Anglos in general dismissed the Penitentes as self-abusing religious crazies.

Fernando moved quietly across the broken flagstone. The morada with its thick adobe walls and buttresses squatted ahead of him in the dark. Moonlight reflected off the side windows and the metal cross on top of the roof. He listened but heard nothing from the house or inside the morada. So he fumbled with the iron latch on the heavy wooden door. At first the door wouldn't budge because it scraped against the flagstone porch. Pulling on the handle with all his strength he managed to yank the door open an inch at a time. Finally he managed to open the door wide enough to squeeze through. Once inside the nave he paused for a moment, feeling the uneven floor of packed clay under his feet. He smelled the biting odor of mold and decay.

A dead animal?

He walked further into the rectangular room guided by the faint light from the windows on either side of the nave. Crucifixes and *retablos* of the saints hung on the walls between windows. Up ahead he saw several pews, most of them broken and pushed to the side. The partition separating the nave from the sanctuary was still intact, though leaning inward. He stood there looking at the sanctuary, amazed that a life-sized wooden crucifix was still standing, covered with dust and cobwebs but still standing. The altar, a narrow table covered with a cloth, held a collection of wooden carvings and tin vessels.

Suddenly out of the corner of his eye Fernando saw the blue light again. It flickered in the room off to his left, the sacristy. Then it moved across the open door of the sacristy from one side to the other. He edged around the partition and moved slowly to the open door. Unlike the nave, the sacristy had only one window on its rear wall. Before entering the near total darkness, he took his cellphone out of his back pocket and clicked on the flashlight app. The narrow beam of light revealed a small, elongated room with a chest of drawers and two ancient trunks along the walls. Further down he saw something bulky in the center of the room.

Using the flashlight he moved forward cautiously. He saw it now, a bulky wooden table with a stone sarcophagus placed on top. He reached out and touched the cold stone coffin. He felt a ridge on the top of the sarcophagus and with his fingers traced the outline of a cross. The symbol had been chipped out of the stone lid. He clicked off his flashlight app and put his cell phone in his pocket. Then he reached out to move the lid aside in order to look inside. He pushed with both hands but the heavy lid wouldn't budge. So he braced his legs and leaned forward, preparing to push with all his weight behind him.

Suddenly the front door of the morada screeched open all the way. The loud sound of the door scraping against the flagstone echoed off the abobe walls. Then he heard voices.

18

"Who's there?" someone shouted from the nave.

Instantly Fernando regretted leaving his weapon in the Cherokee. He waited a second, listening. The footsteps had stopped. Whoever had entered was waiting for him to move or make a noise. He didn't dare use his flashlight app. Feeling his way in the darkness, he moved toward the window in the rear of the sacristy. Though small, the window would be out of sight to anyone in the courtyard or out front of the morada while he made a run for it behind the bungalows.

Moving quickly now Fernando located a *bulto* hanging on the wall, a wooden carving of Saint Francis. He made a point of apologizing to the venerable saint and then carried the *bulto* over to the window and smashed it through the glass. He knew the noise would blow his cover, but there was nothing he could do about that. He had to get out of the morada fast.

Looking around he saw a nearby wooden trunk, which he moved under the window. When he climbed up on the trunk the window was waist high. That allowed him to stick his head and torso out of the window and grab ahold of the trunk of a small aspen tree and pull himself out. Even so he scraped his arms on the bits of jagged glass still attached to the window frame. He let go of the tree as soon as his feet hit the ground. When he landed both his arms were bleeding, so he rubbed them on his pant legs and listened.

"Where'd he go?" someone yelled inside the morada.

"He busted out a window in back!" a second voice said. "I'll go around back to check."

Fernando crept along the side of the morada until he came to the front. Then he peeked around the corner and saw a man holding a baseball bat step outside the front door of the morada. One of the two thugs who worked for Travis.

Turning away, Fernando dashed into the bushes along the arroyo that circled the ranch. He ran blindly until he stumbled over a rock and pitched forward on his hands and knees. The guy with the baseball heard the noise and came after him.

"He's over here—near the arroyo!" the guy shouted and ran into the bushes.

Fernando got to his feet quickly and continued running toward the bungalows. Over his shoulder he saw the second guy come out of the morada carrying a flashlight in one hand and a pistol in the other. Just then a light beam from the flashlight splashed over the bushes in front of him. A shot rang out, clipping the bushes.

Fernando dove behind the first bungalow as a second shot ricocheted off its adobe wall. He picked himself up and moved quickly over to the second bungalow where he had seen Dallas and Jenny earlier.

He paused a moment to glance inside. Dallas sat slumped over in his chair, his chin resting on his chest and his right arm flopped on the table amid the drug paraphernalia. Curiously, Jenny was getting dressed in the bathroom as if she had done her work and was leaving. He wanted to see what Jenny would do next, but he had no time to waste. The flashlight beam flashed on one bungalow after another and then came to rest on the bushes behind him.

Keeping low, Fernando plunged back through the bushes into the arroyo, falling again on his hands and knees. He jumped up quickly and ran over the soft sand in the bottom of the arroyo toward the parking lot and Highway 64.

He heard the two thugs cursing as they waded through the bushes looking for him, splashing the beam of their flashlight in front of them.

Up ahead he saw the arroyo curved around to the left and ran alongside the driveway, so he climbed up the bank of the arroyo and paused a moment to take stock. He saw the flashlight beam moving slowly up the arroyo now, a good fifty yards away. Out of range. Far enough for him to feel safe.

Fernando turned and started jogging down the driveway. The only thing he feared now was the sound of a motor and squealing tires behind him, but none came. When he glimpsed the gray shadow of the highway up ahead, he slowed to a fast walk. He crossed the deserted highway and breathed a sigh of relief when he saw the Cherokee was undisturbed. He climbed in and grabbed his Smith & Wessen, just in case.

He waited to make sure no one had followed him. When he felt satisfied, he placed the Smith & Wessen on the passenger's seat and fired the engine. He took off fast, swiping a bank of chamisa before skidding on loose gravel and bouncing over the lip of the highway. Then he was off.

All the way into Taos Fernando kept looking in the rear view mirror expecting company. Since it was nearly Midnight he considered spending the night in Taos at the El Pueblo, his go-to motor lodge in Taos. But it was too late to call Estelle, and if she woke up tomorrow morning with him missing in action, he would never hear the end of it. She was already pissed that he'd come home so late last night. So at the Plaza he turned south on Highway 68 and headed back to Santa Fe, steeling himself for the long drive. To stay awake he opened the front windows and let the cool bracing air smother him. He gripped the steering wheel tightly with both hands and squeezed intermittently. Like this he drove through the night, cruising along the black ribbon of the Rio Grande with a million stars sparkling in the clear New Mexico sky.

His nerves had started to calm down by the time he reached the outskirts of Española. Now he just felt tired, too tired to drive. He pulled over at the Camel Rock tourist site near Pojoaque and closed his eyes. A big mistake. Because when he opened them again the clock on the dash said three a.m. He got back on the highway and followed it to the first Santa Fe exit. He took the Paseo to Acequia Madre and coasted into his driveway with his lights turned off. He parked at the end of the driveway and walked into the house, trying to be as quiet as he possibly could. He undressed in the living room and tossed his clothes on the sofa. Then he tiptoed down the hall to their master bedroom and crawled into bed next to Estelle. Just as he did Estelle shot upright in the bed.

"Where have you been?" Estelle snapped. "What time is it? Oh my god, it's past three o'clock! This is the second night in a row. Are you having an affair?"

"No!" Fernando said. "I had to go to Taos on business. The Danny Ortiz case I told you about?"

"At this hour? Come on."

"Things got complicated," Fernando said. "Why would I be having an affair?"

"You tell me!" Estelle shot back. "You already had one affair."

Fernando threw up his arms. "That was thirty years ago when I was young. I'm an old man now!"

Estelle looked at him, as if trying to decide if he was too old to have an affair. "Yeah, but old men like young women. You're all alike."

"Estelle, I'm not having an affair," he pleaded. "I'm old, I'm exhausted, I just want to get some sleep."

"Well, then why don't you get some sleep? What's stopping you?"

With that, Estelle lay down and turned her back.

19

Fernando found two messages on his answering machine when he arrived at his office late next morning. The first was from a guy wanting him to investigate a UFO landing last night at Fort Marcy Park. Aliens were pouring out of the UFO like ants, the man reported. Sounded like the man had been drinking, based on his slurred speech and long pauses and the fact that he didn't give his name or phone number. Not to mention the content of his message.

Fernando deleted Mr. UFO. He would take his chances. If a UFO happened to be parked at Fort Marcy and hordes of ant-like aliens were swarming over downtown Santa Fe, well it would be his bad.

The second message was from Paula, asking him to contact her as soon as he could. That surprised him. Did that mean she was still in Santa Fe? Staying at the Residence Inn?

He dialed the number Paula left in her message. She answered immediately.

"Mr. Lopez, thanks for calling back," she said.

"Are you calling from Austin?" he asked.

Paula laughed. "No, I'm still here. I decided to stay with my old boyfriend for a couple of days before going back. I'll probably leave tomorrow morning."

"Aha! So he is better than last time, then?"

"Sort of," she said. "It's complicated. Anyway, I have a message for you. From Scott."

"Scott, the band manager?"

'Yes...he called my cell phone this morning. I'd turned it on to call my boyfriend. He wants to know if he could arrange a meeting with you. He's embarrassed by what happened at the Inn on the Alameda. He wants you to know he had nothing to do with Larry's plan. Basically he just wants to give you his side of the story."

"Really?" Fernando said. "I guess he did seem embarrassed that night. Like he'd rather be elsewhere."

"Scott suggested meeting up at Bishop's Lodge, maybe in the bar or restaurant," she said.

"No, it would have to be someplace more public," Fernando said. "How about the La Fonda Bar at one o'clock this afternoon?"

"Okay, I'll give him your message."

Fernando walked over to El Farol for an early lunch and then decided to stop in at Ruby's gallery next door to chat and kill time.

As he walked to her door he saw Ruby sitting in one of the chairs by the front windows. She gave him the I-see-you sign and laughed.

"What, no business?" Fernando asked as he stepped inside the gallery.

"Nah, I'm just resting," Ruby said. "I had to glaze a couple of pieces at the co-op this morning before coming to the gallery. I didn't even have time to change. I look like death warmed over."

Fernando laughed. Ruby wore her usual jeans and blue shirt with a red scarf tied around her hair, but he didn't see the telltale smudges of potter's clay on her face or clothing.

"So what's up with you?" she asked. "I haven't seen you around lately."

"Yeah, the last couple of days have been crazy. I haven't been in my office much."

"What's the latest on Danny Ortiz?" Ruby asked.

Fernando shrugged. "I'm still not sure who killed him."

Ruby waited for an explanation, so he told her about what he'd found at Painted Skull Ranch, with Dallas maybe held against his will by Travis Walker and the people who beat up Danny when he tried to spring Dallas. Then he told her about the scene at Bishop's Lodge, including Belle's highhanded attitude toward Danny, her husband, and just about everyone else. He also told her about Paula and Larry and the discarded check, followed by their confrontation at the Inn on the Alameda. The entire, tangled story of his investigation..

"Jesus, what a nest of vipers," Ruby said. "I met Belle years ago, back when Dallas was snorting coke with my late, dear husband Jimmy. She was a real bitch. Looked down on everyone. I never understood why Dallas married her. I mean, what's a good old boy from Austin doing with a bitch like that?"

"Opposites attract?" Fernando asked.

Ruby shook her head. "That's bullshit. You want someone you're copacetic with, not someone who doesn't share your values and who you end up fighting with day and night."

"Well, beats me," Fernando said. "It's hard to figure out other people's marriages. Like you and Jimmy."

Ruby gave him the finger.

They laughed and told Jimmy stories until it was time for Fernando to leave for his meeting with Scott. Before leaving he promised to give Ruby an update later that day. Then he climbed into his Cherokee and drove down to Alameda Street. He found a parking spot near the Cathedral and walked the three blocks to La Fonda.

Being cautious, he entered La Fonda through the parking garage and walked slowly down the long hallway to the lobby, past the glittering windows containing expensive merchandise for sale at the hotel shops. Southwestern jewelry and clothing for tourists who wanted a bit of Santa Fe chic to take back home with them. At the end of the hallway he scanned the lobby for any sign of Larry. He didn't want to be surprised in some dark corner of the hotel. Even with one injured arm Larry could be trouble. Scott he wasn't worried about.

Once in the lobby he spotted Scott waving at him from the La Fonda Bar. Scott sat by himself at one of the tables along the rear wall He wore jeans and a denim shirt and was sipping a beer. The relaxed look. Which made Fernando wonder what he wanted.

"Thanks for coming," Scott said as Fernando took a seat at the table.

"How's Larry?" Fernando asked.

Scott shook his head. "You were right, he needed surgery on his arm. But he's healing. His right arm's in a sling. Doctors tell him he'll be as good as new in about six weeks."

Fernando watched Scott closely, trying to get a read.

"That's why I asked to meet you," Scott said. "To apologize, really. I wanted to let you know I had nothing to do with the way Larry treated Paula. I like Paula. Larry should never have laid a hand on her. Belle sent me along with him to make sure he didn't hurt her any more than he had. That's the truth."

"So where were you when he was manhandling her?" Fernando interrupted his monologue.

"I tried to stop him, I really did," Scott said.

Just then a bartender came around the bar and ambled over to their table. Fernando recognized Morris, who he'd known for years. Heavy-set with a black handlebar mustache, Morris looked like an old time bandito. "Can I get you something, Fernando?" he asked.

Fernando checked his watch. "What the hell. Give me a Modelo."

"You got it," Morris said and ambled back to the bar. Morris didn't move fast for anyone.

When his beer came, Fernando took a long drink and then asked, "What about the torn check Paula found in Larry's wastebasket? The check Dallas wrote to Danny Ortiz for a thousand dollars. Do you know anything about that?"

Scott shook his head. "Larry went out the night Donny was murdered. He wouldn't say where he'd been. But when he came back he tore up the check Dallas had written and tossed it in the trash. I have no idea where or how he got his hands on the check."

"Are you sure you weren't with him that night?" Fernando asked.

"No, I stayed in the casita with Belle. She'll confirm that."

"Did you see anyone else with Larry that night?"

"Well..." Scott paused for a moment. "I saw him drinking at the Bishop's Lodge bar earlier with some guys I'd never see before."

"So they were strangers?"

"I guess," Scott said. "Unless they were staff. Some of the servers like to stay for a drink or two after their shifts end. I've only met a few of them."

Fernando nodded.

"So that's what I wanted you to know," Scott said. "Our team will be breaking up soon so I thought I might not get another chance to talk with you."

"Breaking up?"

"Yes, as soon as we get back to Austin," Scott said. "Belle is letting all of us go. She's already fired Paula. You heard what she said the other day. She's divorcing Dallas and taking her share of their wealth before he can waste it all."

Fernando was skeptical. "Tell me, can Dallas really be as bad as she makes him out to be?"

"Absolutely," Scott said. "He hasn't been able to perform a concert in over six months. He had a melt-down last fall in Amarillo. He forgot what he was doing and started mumbling onstage. We had to go out and physically help him off stage. It was a disaster. We had to reimburse the audience and do damage control with all the Texas media. Everyone was embarrassed. Everyone except Dallas. You can imagine Belle's reaction."

"Is it dementia...or all the drugs he's taken over the years?" Fernando asked point blank.

Scott shrugged. "Probably both. I don't really know."

"So what'll happen to Dallas?" Fernando asked.

"I imagine he'll end up living with one of his drinking buddies or druggies, at least for the short term," Scott said.

"What about long term?" Fernando asked.

Scott laughed. "Well, Belle certainly won't be looking after him. And I don't think he can take care of himself. He certainly can't manage his own finances. So I suppose eventually he'll have to go into some sort of assisted living situation."

"Seems kind of harsh...for a man of his stature, don't you think?"

Scott raised his hands. "What are you going to do?"

The question hung in the air as they finished their beers.

Neither of them had anything else to say.

Scott stood up. "Again, thanks for meeting me."

Fernando nodded and held up his hand. He watched Scott walk out of the bar into the La Fonda lobby and disappear through the doors on San Francisco Street, his performance concluded.

20

Fernando drove back to his office on Canyon Road feeling uneasy about Scott. Suspicious by nature, he was skeptical of Scott's motive for wanting to talk. Why now? It was clear that Scott was a professional salesman. Fernando just couldn't quite figure out what exactly the young man was selling and who had sent him. Had Belle sent him on a mission to mislead? To dis-inform? He wished he'd asked Paula for more information about Scott. Maybe he would give her a call later.

When he walked into his office he noticed the light on his desk phone. Another message. He sat at his desk and hit the replay button.

"Where the hell are you?" came blaring out of the speaker. Hank's voice. Not a good sign.

He hit the redial button. Hank answered immediately.

"What's up?" Fernando asked.

"Where you been...haven't you heard the news?" Hank asked. "Dallas Longstreet died this morning. That young fella with stringy red hair who works for Travis Walker found him dead in his bungalow. Looks like an overdose. Forensics just took the body away. I got television news trucks and reporters from all the daily newspapers in northern New Mexico up here. The place is a damn zoo!"

Stunned, Fernando didn't know what to say.

"So are you coming up?" Hank asked.

"I don't know, I just got back from Taos last night," Fernando said. "I was there at the ranch. I tried again to get Dallas to leave."

"Well, in that case you best come up," Hank said. "If you saw him last night we'll need to get your statement."

Fernando sighed. "Okay, I'll be there as soon as I can."

As soon as he hung up on Hank he called Estelle and explained what had happened and that he needed to go back to Taos. She seemed to understand, given the gravity of the situation. Then he drove home and picked up his overnight bag, just a change of clothes and his shaving kit.

He'd learned the hard way that it was better to be prepared in case he had to spend the night.

On the way out of town Fernando stopped at the Sunoco station and gassed up the Cherokee. He bought a couple bottles of water at the counter and then hit the road. Once again he found himself on Highway 285 North, the familiar signs flashing by as if he were in a dream that kept reoccurring: Tesuque, Santa Fe Opera, Pojoaque, Nambe, Española. All the way to Taos he kept thinking about what Dallas had said about Belle: "My wife is trying to kill me."

Fernando struggled with the familiar feelings of guilt and regret. He should have done more to help Dallas. To get him away from the ranch. Somehow.

At the Plaza he turned right on Kit Carson and followed it past the Mabel Dodge Luhan House to where it became Highway 64. Approaching the ranch he saw a *Santa Fe Independent* car parked at the end of the driveway. A photographer from the newspaper who he didn't recognize walked around the totem pole shooting photographs of the painted skull for tomorrow's paper. The media loved the macabre detail, the sensational element that sold the story. He gritted his teeth and pulled in beside the other car.

Fernando stepped out of the Cherokee and walked toward the totem pole. As he did the driver's window of the *Independent* car buzzed down.

"Hey, Fernando, I haven't seen you in a while," said someone behind the wheel. The voice was familiar.

He turned to see Fidel Rodriguez, an old friend from his days as a detective, sitting in the driver's seat. Fidel was one of the few *Independent* reporters he actually liked.

Fernando had to laugh when he saw Fidel wearing the same thing he always wore: a blue shirt and paisley tie. His reporter's uniform.

"What are you doing up here?" Fidel asked.

"Working on a case," Fernando said. "Trying to find out who killed Danny Ortiz. And trying to get Dallas out of here and into rehab."

Fidel nodded. "Yeah, it's a nasty scene in there. They're saying he overdosed, but I don't know, it looks staged to me."

That took Fernando by surprise. "What do you mean?"

"Well, Dallas was sprawled over a kitchen table with needles and dime packets of white powder spread out in front of him, all neatly arranged. Made it look like he was picking and choosing from a drug smorgasbord. I don't know. It was just too neat for the scene of an overdose. In my opinion."

"Is that what you're going to write?" Fernando asked.

"No! Are you kidding?" Fidel asked, laughing. "The paper wants a celebration of the life of a country-rock legend. They're giving me half a page. They don't want any mention of foul play even if I could get anyone to go on record with that suggestion, which I can't."

When Fernando didn't respond, Fidel yelled at his photographer. "Let's go. I got a deadline tonight!"

"Okay, boss!" the photographer said. A young woman wearing a huge Nikon around her neck, she scurried over to Fidel's car and climbed into the front passenger's seat. She slammed the car door and immediately began looking over the digital photos she'd taken.

Before leaving, Fidel stuck his head out of the car window and said, "I'll tell you more when the smoke clears."

Fernando watched Fidel speed off on Highway 64 toward Taos and Santa Fe. When their car disappeared over the horizon he climbed into the Cherokee and drove down to the ranch parking lot, where the crew of a KQRE News 13 van was in the process of lowering its broadcast antenna and packing up its cameras. A TV reporter was standing by the van checking her notes.

Fernando parked between two cruisers belonging to the Taos County Sheriff. By the time he stepped out of the Cherokee the news van was already headed out to the highway.

He started down the flagstone walkway. Down by the courtyard he saw Jerry sitting on a bench with his head bowed. Not too far away stood a deputy sheriff named Roy, a young guy who he'd only met once last year.

"Howdy," Roy said as Fernando approached.

"Hey, Roy, what's the situation?"

"Well, it's been a long day," Roy said, a short but powerfully built cop with a buzzed haircut. "Jerry here found Dallas this morning. We were on our way over because the search warrant was finally approved. We didn't know Dallas was dead until we arrived. So we called forensics right away and searched the ranch while forensics took care of the body. Somehow the media got wind of Dallas' death and showed up here like a bunch of damn vultures, one after another. The parking lot was full of vans and cars from Santa Fe and Albuquerque. Things have calmed down a bit now."

Jerry sunk even lower on the bench, holding his head in his hands now.

"What did you find in the search?" Fernando asked.

"No illegal drugs except the heroin Dallas had in his casita. Looks like an overdose."

Fernando nodded. "That's what Hank said. Where is Hank?"

Roy motioned toward the house. "He's in the house with Travis Walker and the others."

"Thanks," Fernando said, and walked over to where Jerry was sitting. "Are you okay?"

Jerry raised his head. His red stringy hair looked like it hadn't been washed in weeks. "I got fired. I don't know why Mister Walker would blame me for Mister Longstreet's death. I just found him this morning when I went to his casita to bring clean towels. Why would Mister Walker blame me?"

"No, I'm sure he doesn't blame you for what happened to Dallas," Fernando said. "Maybe he doesn't need you right now because there aren't many guests staying here. Plus the bad publicity from this can't be good for business. I'd imagine people will be staying away."

Jerry nodded. "Maybe. All I know is that I was Mister Bill's caretaker at the ranch for the past ten years. He never fired me."

Fernando paused when he heard this. "You were Bill Candelaria's caretaker?"

Jerry nodded. "He was a good man. He helped me and my dad out lots of times. He never fired me."

Fernando didn't respond.

"Here," Jerry said, handing him a folded slip of paper.

"What is it?" Fernando asked. When Jerry didn't respond, he tucked the paper in his rear pocket to view later, not wanting to take the time now.

Fernando walked up the flagstone patio to the house to look for Hank. Inside the kitchen he heard voices in the rear of the house. He walked down the hallway, past the empty bedrooms, into the last sitting room with the shepherd's fireplace along one wall. Hank stood in the center of the room, gesturing and pacing while he talked to Travis and a woman sitting on the Taos sofa. Fernando did a double-take on the woman, who looked familiar. Then it clicked. The woman was none other than Jenny, but not cowgirl Jenny. This Jenny wore a nurse's uniform with her hair in a tight bun on top, very professional.

Fernando shook his head, hardly believing his eyes. Clearly, cowgirl Jenny was just an act, but to what purpose? To entrap Dallas?

Hank nodded when Fernando entered the room and then turned back to Travis and Jenny. "So you're telling me Dallas himself brought all the needles and dime bags forensics cleared out of that casita? I find that damn hard to believe."

"Absolutely," Travis said, sounding exasperated. "As I keep telling you, the only drug we sell here is marijuana, because it's legal in New Mexico. You've already searched the ranch and found nothing, so why do you keep asking me the same question?"

A pained, sorrowful look came over Hank's face. "Well, sir, I'll tell you why." He paused for effect, shaking his head sadly. "The man's wife Belle happens to be down at the morgue right now with my deputy Dave. She tells us that Dallas never had any drugs in his possession before he came up to the ranch. That he'd been clean for several years."

"She said that?" Travis shot back. His face turned red with anger. "The bitch said that?"

Hank nodded. "Deed she did. And as for not finding your drugs, well it's a big ole ranch and it's gonna take us some time, but we will find them, I guarantee you that. So you might wanna rethink your attitude, fella. Tell us where you hid them now and I'll do my damnedest to cut you a deal. The D.A. has been known to let worse offenders than yourself go scot free. But you need to get that burr out of your saddle and cooperate. You understand?"

Travis glared at Hank, not responding.

Hank turned to Jenny. "What about you, sister? Last time I was here you were all over Dallas, noodling him. Were you with him last night or this morning when he OD'd?"

Jenny shook her head, very composed. "No, I didn't see him at all yesterday or this morning."

"That's a lie," Fernando interjected, stepping forward. "I saw you in Dallas' casita last night. You were in his bed half naked. Maybe shooting up with him, I couldn't tell."

"No. You're mistaken," Jenny responded, her voice as cold as ice. "I was never there. Must have been someone else you saw."

"Jenny's a professional, she would never take drugs with a known addict," Travis added.

Hank shook his head sadly. "Okay, have it your way. You're digging your own graves, the both of you."

With that Hank turned and walked out on the porch.

Fernando followed, noticing the two toughs who worked for Travis sitting together on the bench. They both looked worried.

Hank checked his pocket notebook for their names. "Well, well, Hal Lars and Tony Taponga. We had our boys back at the station run your names. Seems both of you have rap sheets as long as my arm. Given that, tell me how in the hell did you end up working for a drug dealer?"

"When you've done time it ain't easy to find a job," said the smaller of the two, wearing dirty jeans and a khaki shirt. "I'm Hal."

"I know who you are," Hank said.

The bigger of the two, the one who walked around with balled fists, scowled silently at the proceedings.

"You," Hank said and pointed to the big guy. "Why don't you tell us where the drugs are hidden. You cooperate, and the D.A. will likely cut you a sweet deal. Keep you out of prison. You don't wanna go back to the big house, do you?"

Tony ignored Hank. He stared straight ahead, refusing to even look at Hank or Fernando.

"Don't send us back to prison, sheriff," Hal said. "We're just hired hands. We do whatever Travis tell us to do. It's a living, that's all it is."

Fernando stepped forward. "What about the shipment you picked up earlier in the week at the Albuquerque train station? What happened to that?"

Hal sighed. "We helped him bring the shipment back, but Travis took it from there. I don't know what he did with it. He doesn't tell us those things. Like I said, we're just peons."

Hank smiled. "So everyone says. Well, you boys stick around in case we need your statements down at the station. If you try to run, I'll put you in jail for a long time while you wait for your day in court. Understand?"

Hal glanced at Tony and then nodded. Tony scowled at all of them.

21

Fernando and Hank stood in the parking lot overlooking Painted Skull Ranch. The other visitors had departed, including Roy and all the media types who were there earlier. Roy had joined Dave at Holy Cross Hospital, where Dallas' body was in the process of being transferred to OMI, the New Mexico Office of the Medical Examiner in Albuquerque. OMI would determine the official cause of death.

Hank removed his Stetson and wiped his sweaty face with a kerchief.

"Now what?" Fernando asked.

Hank shrugged. "We'll know more when we get the forensics report. Fingerprints and DNA on all the drug odds and ends found in the dead man's casita. In the meantime we need to find Travis' stash of drugs. They must be somewhere on the grounds hereabouts."

Fernando checked his watch. "It's already past five. You want to meet me at Michael's Kitchen for dinner? Looks like I might have to spend the night at El Pueblo again."

"Good. That way we can get an early start tomorrow morning looking for the drugs," Hank said.

Hank left first. He roared off fast in his cruiser, sliding out of the gravel parking lot and tearing down the drive to the highway. The man was always in a hurry. Or late, depending on how you looked at it.

On the other hand Fernando took his time. He was already thinking about what he would tell Estelle. Another night in Taos. She wouldn't be happy.

He waited until Hank's dust had settled in the driveway before following. At the end of the driveway he stopped next to the totem pole and climbed out of the Cherokee. He couldn't help himself. He had to know if the painted skull on top of the pole was in fact human. He walked to the pole and reached up to touch the skull. It felt and looked real to him, even the few teeth that remained on the lower jaw. The skull's empty eye sockets were painted a deep red, which made it look like the skull was bleeding out. Almost alive.

Satisfied the skull was human, Fernando jumped back in the Cherokee and drove into Taos. He turned right on the Paseo and then two blocks later left into the parking lot next to Michael's Kitchen. He saw Hank waiting for him on the bench in front of Michael's.

"Hey Hank," the cashier said as they walked into Michael's. Since his wife died, Hank had been a regular customer at Michael's. Everyone knew him.

"Follow me, Hank," said an older woman with gray hair and glasses. "We have your favorite table ready for you."

They followed her to a corner table in the back of the room.

"Thanks, Doreen," Hank said, removing his Stetson and placing it carefully on the back of a chair.

"Can I get you boys something to drink?" Doreen asked.

"Hah! Can you ever. Been a long day."

"I'll have a Modelo," Fernando said.

"Make that two," Hank added.

Doreen returned quickly with their beers. "Do you fellas want your usuals? Chicken dinner for Hank, and for you I seem to remember the enchilada plate red," she said to Fernando.

"Damn, are we that predictable?" Hank asked, nodding yes.

Doreen laughed. "Most are. At least those who come in here." She hurried off to the kitchen.

"So, what's your plan for tomorrow?" Fernando asked when they were alone.

Hank shook his head. "I don't really have a plan. You think we could get any of the others to turn on Travis?"

"Yeah, I thought maybe Jenny would cooperate back when she appeared to be a simple cowgirl," Fernando said. "But seeing her today in a nurse's uniform and knowing she works for Travis, I doubt it. Hal and Tony, no way. Maybe Jerry, the gangly little guy with red hair. Apparently Travis fired him. Jerry seems to think Travis blames him for Dallas Longstreet's overdose. Why, I don't know."

"No shit? Why Jerry? How was he involved with Dallas?"

"He wasn't, as far as I know. Except that he found the body."

Hank nodded.

"Speaking of Jerry, he slipped me a folded piece of paper back at the ranch. I forgot about that."

Fernando pulled the paper out of his back pocket and unfolded it. He read the handwritten note and then paused. Then he read it again.

"Well, what's it say?" Hank asked, impatient to know.

Fernando read the note out loud: "Check out the old ranch dump behind the house. Just follow the dirt road from the parking lot around behind the morada. Look in the arroyo."

Hank opened his hands. "Is he talking about illegal drugs? Why would Travis keep his drug supply in a dump?"

"He wouldn't...would he?"

Neither of them had an answer to that, so when Doreen returned they ordered another round of beers and discussed a plan for tomorrow. They agreed that Hank would pick up Fernando around nine o'clock at the El Pueblo.

After they finished dinner, Hank headed home and Fernando bit the bullet and drove a block up to the El Pueblo, which had become his go-to place to stay in Taos. He parked the Cherokee next to the office and walked inside.

"Why, Fernando Lopez, I'll be...." said a familiar face behind the counter.

Fernando laughed. He recognized the man in the Mr. Rogers sweater and glasses from his last stay. The man had put on a few pounds but otherwise looked the same. Big smile, friendly attitude.

"What brings you back so soon?"

"Another case—I'm a private investigator," Fernando said. He handed the man his card. "I'm sorry, I don't know your name."

"Name's Mike," the man replied. "So do you want the weekly rate again? It's cheaper."

Fernando laughed. "No, just one night this time. Give me the end unit again."

"You got it."

Fernando took the keycard and walked outside. He never imagined being back at the El Pueblo so soon, but here he was. He moved the Cherokee over in front of his room and carried his duffel bag inside. He tossed the duffel bag on the closest of the two queen beds.

The room smelled stale, so he opened the front windows and left the door open for a few minutes while he paced back and forth in the room, deciding whether to call or text Estelle. He wanted to avoid another argument, so he sat down in the stuffed chair and sent her a text explaining that he would have to stay in Toas overnight but should be home tomorrow afternoon.

Should was the operative word. That left him leeway for whatever happened tomorrow.

Being back at the El Pueblo put him in a reflective mood. Somehow his investigation into the murder of Danny Ortiz had gotten off track and he'd fallen into the orbit of Dallas Longstreet and all his problems. By happenstance, not by intention.

For days now he'd delayed calling Oralia. Partly because he couldn't say for sure who had murdered her husband. So far the evidence pointed to Larry, who had the motive and the violent temperament.

With his cell phone in his hand he started to dial Oralia. Just as quickly he changed his mind and clicked off. Instead of calling, he sat in the chair brooding.

22

Fernando watched the Taos County Sheriff's cruiser turn into the El Pueblo parking lot at half past nine. He had been waiting in the metal chair out front of his room for thirty minutes. Hank drove, while Roy rode shotgun. That made three of them, not nearly enough hands and feet to search a ranch as large as Painted Skull. Unless, of course, Travis had in fact hidden his drugs in the old dump. Which seemed highly unlikely.

Hank eased his cruiser into the parking space next to the Cherokee and rolled down his window. "You ready?"

Fernando stepped down from the porch. "You sure you don't want to take my Cherokee? Those dirt roads can be rough going."

"Nah, let's make sure they understand it's an official visit," Hank said.

Fernando climbed into the rear seat behind Roy. Roy nodded.

Hank backed out of the tight parking space and then turned the cruiser loose. He hit the brake before turning right on the Paseo and then shot ahead to the Kit Carson intersection and turned left.

Hank glanced back at Fernando. "I told Roy about the note from Jerry. So we'll check the dump first."

Roy laughed. "As if anyone would hide drugs in a damn dump!"

"Still, there must be some reason why Jerry told us to check out the dump," Fernando said.

Hank did not respond. None of them spoke another word on the ride to Painted Skull Ranch. Not until they turned into the driveway.

Hank stopped at the totem pole and stared at the skull on top. "There oughta be a law," he said finally and then gunned the big cruiser. The cruiser left a thick cloud of dust behind them.

"There's the road," Fernando said, pointing to the left.

Hank slowed to a stop. "I see it on the other side of the arroyo. We need to find a place to cross over."

"Down there where it's flat. You can see the tire tracks," Roy said, pointing to a bend in the arroyo.

Hank saw it too. He turned sharply and followed the tracks into the arroyo, the tires of the cruiser beginning to spin in the soft sand. In response Hank shifted into reverse and lurched back a few feet. Then he shifted into drive and hit the gas pedal and tried again to get traction in the deep sand. The cruiser careened forward a couple of feet and then stopped. No luck.

"You boys are gonna have to get out and push," Hank said. "Just till we get across the arroyo. The road looks fine."

Fernando and Roy climbed out of the cruiser and walked through the soft sand to the rear of the vehicle. They pushed as soon as Hank hit the gas pedal. The heavy cruiser bucked and jerked its way incrementally across the bottom of the arroyo. Finally the tires caught on firm ground and the cruiser jumped over the lip of the arroyo onto the dirt road. Hank slammed on the brakes.

Fernando and Roy looked at each other and laughed. They were covered head to foot with red dust and sand. It took them a few minutes to brush off their clothes and shake the sand out of their hair.

With grains of sand gritty between his teeth, Fernando spit.

"Sorry about that, boys," Hank said as he watched them climb into the cruiser. "I'll get out and push next time."

"Sure you will," Roy said and shot Hank a dirty look.

Hank shrugged and eased the cruiser forward. The narrow road followed the shallow, twisting arroyo downhill. They passed the collapsed sheds and the bungalows and approached the morada. Here the road turned to the right and curved around behind the morada and the main house.

Suddenly Hank slammed on the brakes. "Whoa!"

"Christ!" Roy said. Roy threw open his door after the cruiser skidded to a stop on the road. He followed Hank to the lip of the arroyo.

From the back seat Fernando couldn't see the problem. Only when he stepped out of the cruiser and joined the others did he see the macabre sight. The arroyo behind the morada had cut deeply into the campo santo, splitting the earth wide open and badly damaging the small graveyard. Several entire graves had collapsed into the arroyo leaving crosses and headstones scrambled every which way. Bleached human bones littered the bottom of the arroyo—ribs, arms, legs, and skulls, some of them partially buried in the sand.

"Maybe this is where the painted skull on the totem pole came from," Fernando said.

Hank shook his head. "It ain't right. You can't let this happen to a cemetery. I can't believe old Bill would let it go to hell like this. I mean, these are his relatives buried here."

"Downright disrespectful," Roy added.

They stood at the edge of the arroyo staring at the exposed bones. Fernando counted three skulls, two without jawbones.

"Okay, let's move on—do what we came to do and get the hell out of here," Hank said finally. "I'll have to report this. The Department of Health might have to get involved. Hell, for all I know this might be a violation of the Native American Graves Protection Act. Just what I don't need right now, having to deal with the Feds. Goddammit to hell."

Hank led the way back to the cruiser. Fernando and Roy followed, glancing back at the bones in the arroyo. Something you didn't see every day.

Hank eased back on the road, proceeding slowly. They followed the arroyo over the mesa, through sage and snake grass and the occasional clumps of cactus. Up ahead the foothills appeared, dotted with gnarly piñon and juniper trees. They'd gone about a quarter mile when the road climbed steeply. Almost immediately the cruiser's tires began to spin in the sand, unable to get traction uphill in the soft sand.

Hank turned to look at Roy and Fernando. "You boys know I'd help if I didn't have bad arthritis in my knees. I sure enough would."

Roy laughed and climbed out of the cruiser. Fernando followed, not bothering to argue.

Once again the two of them pushed from behind as Hank tried rocking the cruiser back and forth to get unstuck. This time nothing worked because they were pushing uphill.

Covered with sweat and sand, Fernando leaned against the cruiser to catch his breath. Roy did the same.

Hank waved at them to stop. "Well, to hell with it. Let's walk the rest of the way. We'll worry about the car after we check out the dump."

"Good idea," Roy said, trying to wipe sand from his eyes.

Hank led the way with Roy and Fernando following. They saw more arroyo cutting the farther they walked, with jagged channels branching off in myriad directions, some with collapsing banks.

Favoring his knees, Hank quickly fell behind. By the time Fernando and Roy sighted the ranch dump Hank was a good twenty yards behind them.

The old dump totally filled a deep, dead-end branch of the arroyo. Crumbling adobes, rotting lumber, scrap metal, rusted tin roofing, and a rounded pile of ancient cans and bottles came into view first. Busted glass littered the roadside. As they came closer they began to smell smoke, or rather the burned out remains of whatever it was that had burned.

"What the fuck?" Roy muttered, the first to arrive.

"What is it?" Hank asked, hobbling as fast as he could.

Fernando pointed over the edge of the arroyo.

The three of them stood looking down at the torched remains of a small sedan. Its tires had melted and its insides had burned to bare metal. Nothing remained but the blackened shell of the automobile.

23

"So that's what Jerry wanted us to see," Fernando said.

Hank frowned. "You guys go down and check it out. My knees won't get me down there. Or back up."

Roy gave Hank another dirty look.

Tire tracks led to the lip of the arroyo, where the car had been driven or pushed over. Fernando went first, digging his heels into the side of the arroyo as he tried to navigate the twenty-foot drop. Halfway down his feet slipped out from under him and he slid the rest of the way on his ass before sprawling on his hands and knees in the sand. Roy met the same fate, landing face down in the sand.

Fernando dusted himself off, while Roy stood up and spat, trying to get the sand out of his mouth. Up close the smell of the burned vehicle was overpowering. Fragments of glass littered the area like jagged black pebbles.

Fernando held his breath while he inspected the car. All the plastic inside the cab had melted like wax. The upholstery had combusted without a trace. What remained of the front seats were springs attached to the bare metal floor. The rear seats looked the same. To create a fire this intense you had to use gasoline. A whole lot of gasoline.

"Tell me, do you see any human remains?" Hank asked, peering down from the top of the arroyo.

"No," Fernando said. "No charred bones. No bits of shoes. Nothing that I can see."

Meanwhile Roy circled the outside of the small car. He ran his fingers over the fenders and doors, leaving his fingers black with soot.

When he came to the front of the car Roy stopped to examine something. He took out a pocket knife and scraped away soot and residue. "Hey, look at this. It's the Mercedes emblem—the three-pointed star. This is a fucking Mercedes. What a waste!"

Fernando came around front to see. He ran his hand over the blackened emblem and nodded. Then he looked lower at the bent, charred license plate and ran his hand over that. The tag and the lettering had been obliterated, but he could feel the raised letters with his fingers. He traced a C and then an O and stopped there. He didn't need to go any further.

"The car has a Colorado license plate," Fernando announced.

"No shit? You sure? Colorado?" Hank asked.

Roy stood back from the car. He had no idea what to make of their reaction to the Colorado plate.

"Well, I'll be go to hell," Hank said. "No wonder they can't find old Bill Candelaria in Pueblo. He's here. Or was."

"That's what Jerry was trying to tell us," Fernando said. "He said he worked as Candelaria's caretaker for ten years and that he liked working for the man. This was his way of showing us what happened to Candelaria."

Hank shook his head from side to side and then sighed. "Well, make damned sure there's no human remains. Look around the vehicle—see what you can find. Maybe they threw the body in separately."

Fernando and Roy spread out into the dump, climbing over piles of rubble, broken glass, and scrap metal. Fernando found the broken handle of a garden implement, either a rake or a hoe, and used that to stir the loose garbage. They spent about thirty minutes overturning and wading through the mound of trash but turned up no evidence of human remains. The only thing they did turn up was a nest of rats that scampered out of their reach.

"Watch out for the fucking rats," Roy said. "They carry the plague."

Hank walked along the top of the arroyo giving orders and asking questions. "Do you see any other ashes? Maybe they burned the body elsewhere and tossed the ashes here."

"No, I don't see any ashes or burned remains," Fernando said. "Nothing like that."

Fernando stopped for a moment and tossed aside his broken handle. He wiped his forehead with a kerchief. The sun was directly overhead in a steel blue sky. Looked like it was going to be an unseasonably hot day, too hot to be searching through a dump for a dead body.

Suddenly it occurred to him. Like a news flash.

"Wait," Fernando said. "I think I might know where we can find Bill Candelaria."

"Where?" Hank asked, pausing for a moment on the lip of the arroyo.

Instead of answering, Fernando climbed up the bank of the arroyo using exposed roots to pull himself up. Roy did the same.

"Follow me," Fernando said. He turned and started walking back down the road to the ranch. Hank and Roy followed.

"You wanna tell me what the hell's going on?" Hank asked but Fernando didn't respond.

They walked down the winding dirt road to the cruiser. When Hank's cell phone rang the big man stopped in front of his cruiser and leaned against the hood to rest. "Mathews here."

Hank listened while Fernando and Roy waited.

"No shit," Hank said. "Okay then. I'll get back to you as soon as we're done here."

Hank pocketed his phone and turned to them. "That was deputy Dave. He called to let us know they just now sent Dallas' body to OMI in Albuquerque so the medical investigator can make the final determination. But that ain't all. Seems Belle Longstreet told Dave where Travis keeps his drugs."

"Hah! I can't say I'm surprised," Fernando said, beginning to understand the larger picture.

"She says the trastero in his office has a false back," Hank said. "The drugs are there, locked in a sealed metal container. If true, we might have enough to charge that sonofabitch even if we don't find Bill!"

"Good. That saves us a lot of trouble searching for the drugs," Fernando said.

Meanwhile, Roy placed small rocks under the rear tires of the cruiser and then turned to Hank. "I think we can get this unstuck if we push from the front. You wanna try now?"

Hank looked at Fernando.

"Let's find Bill first," Fernando said. "I think I know where he is."

Fernando walked along the arroyo until he found a reasonably flat place to cross. That turned out to be behind the morada, where the campo santo had partially collapsed into the arroyo. He climbed down the bank of the arroyo and followed a trail of animal tracks crossing over to the other side. He stepped lightly in the sand, careful to avoid the bleached white bones that littered the bottom of the arroyo. He dodged one human skull with its jawbone wide open as if indulging in one last scream.

"For God's sake, don't mess with the bones," Hank said. "My late wife always said that was the best way to get the ghosts riled up."

Roy followed Hank into the arroyo. "Didn't know you were superstitious."

"I'm not. I just don't want to rile up no ghosts."

Roy gave Hank a funny look.

Fernando reached the far side of the arroyo and climbed up the bank. His feet slipped in the loose sand. Once on top he stood among the crosses that had been scrambled by erosion and arroyo-cutting. He waited for Hank, giving him a hand up as he crested the lip of the arroyo. Then Roy.

They walked through the graveyard to the back of the morado.

Fernando paused a moment, taking cover behind one of the rear buttresses that bolstered the thick adobe walls. He listened for a moment but heard nothing. He saw no one in the courtyard.

"Follow me," Fernando said, and moved out from behind the buttress. He led them to the front door of the morada, which was padlocked now, unlike the first time he'd entered.

While the others joined him, Fernando took out his lock pick and opened the padlock, tossing it on the ground.

They entered the dark morada one at a time, letting their eyes adjust to the darkness. The statuary hanging on the walls and placed in the indented nichos looked ominous in the dark.

Hank muttered out loud as he bumped into one of the overturned pews. He stood frozen, glaring at the life-size crucifix behind the altar. Light from a side window slashed bars through the crucifix.

"This way," Fernando said. He grabbed Hank's sleeve and pulled him toward the door to the sacristy. Roy followed behind.

Once in the more secluded sacristy Fernando grabbed his cell phone and clicked on the flashlight app. A feeble light splashed on the dusty floor ahead of him. In the shadows he saw the hulking sarcophagus lying on its table. He moved closer and then stopped, waiting for Roy to join them in the sacristy.

"This place stinks to high heaven. Is there a dead animal in here somewhere?" Roy asked.

Fernando didn't bother to respond. Instead he shined his light on the sarcophagus so the others could see the stone receptacle. "You see? I need your help to open this thing. The top just slides off. I think."

So the three of them positioned themselves, Hank and Roy at the ends and Fernando in the middle of the sarcophagus. They pushed together, barely budging the massive lid.

"Harder. Use your whole body," Fernando said.

They tried again. This time the lid moved slightly, as stone scraped against stone. They pushed again, this time too hard. The damned thing slid so far they lost the center of gravity. Fernando tried to grab the lid as it fell over the top of the sarcophagus but it was far too heavy. When it hit, the brittle stone exploded on the floor, sending a hundred pieces crashing against the wall behind it. The sound was deafening. Like an echo chamber.

Hank cursed. "Now that we've alerted the whole fucking place, let's make this quick."

Fernando obliged. He held his cell phone over the open sarcophagus. The pale white light revealed the body of an elderly man with thin white hair. Looked like he'd been dead for some time. His face had turned a yellowish black color. The skin had shrunk around his open mouth exposing his teeth. His open eyes were empty sockets. His chest was stained black from bullet holes in the center of his shirt. His identity was not much of a mystery.

"Jesus, what's that underneath the body?" Hank said.

Fernando adjusted the light. Underneath the body lay a skeleton—the remains of an ancient burial.

"Wait, the skull's missing," Hank said.

"So then maybe this was the skull they took for the totem pole," Fernando said. "They could have taken it when they put Candelaria in the sarcophagus."

"Goddamn skulls everywhere around here," Hank muttered.

Roy spun around and retched on the floor.

"Yeah, old Bill stinks like a sonofabitch," Hank said, shaking his head. He turned to Fernando. "How'd you know he was here?"

"I saw a light."

Hank cocked his eye. "What the hell does that mean?"

"I saw a light when I poked around in here a couple of days ago," Fernando said. "Like a cloud of smoke, except bright. It led me into the sacristy and right to the sarcophagus."

Hank nodded. "Are you saying you saw Bill's ghost?"

"Something like that," Fernando said. "I don't know what it was, only that it took me right to the sarcophagus. Like it wanted me to find the body."

"So it could be properly buried?" Hank asked.

Fernando shrugged.

"What a way for the family to end," Hank mused, peering into the sarcophagus again.

Eager to leave before Travis could send over Hal and Tony, Fernando changed the subject. "Looks like you have the evidence you need."

"Yeah. Let's get the hell out of here and call forensics," Hank said. "Let them deal with the body."

Roy stumbled into the wall on his way out, desperate to get some fresh air.

"But be careful, goddamnit!" Hank yelled at Roy. "We don't know who's outside that door."

They heard Roy stumbling into the pews in the nave. Then opening the heavy wooden door.

Suddenly a series of explosions sounded outside.

POP! POP! POP!

24

Fernando ran for the door, stumbling against one of the broken pews. He kicked the pew out of the way and dashed to the door. Just outside Roy lay on the flagstone walkway holding his right thigh. Blood oozed between his fingers and pooled on the ground. Without thinking, Fernando fell on his hands and knees and shimmied outside. He grabbed Roy under the shoulders and dragged him inside the door out of harm's way.

"I'm bleeding," Roy moaned.

Fernando ripped off his belt and tightened it around Roy's leg above the wound. The blood flow lessened and finally stopped. He turned to Hank and said, "Call for an ambulance."

Nodding, Hank was already on the phone calling the station. "They're on their way. They'll be here soon."

Fernando studied the lay of the land. He spotted the shooter crouching behind a bench up near the back patio. It looked like Tony, the bigger of the two hired hands. So where was Hal?

Fernando waited, watching for any movement around the morada. Finally he noticed a couple of birds fluttering out of the courtyard squawking. That told him Hal was hiding somewhere in the overgrown courtyard. Up on the porch Travis watched the action from the protection one of the massive wooden beams that held up the roof. Both Tony and Travis carried handguns. Fernando didn't know about Hal.

"How do you wanna play this?" Hank asked, from behind Fernando.

"We need to move fast, Roy's lost a lot of blood," Fernando said. "Stay here. I'll climb out the broken window in the sacristy and circle around to the courtyard. I'll take care of whichever one is in the courtyard. When the other one comes out from behind the bench, shoot him. Okay?"

"Oh, I plan to shoot him all right, you just take care of the other one," Hank said, smiling.

He trusted Hank. The best shot with a pistol he'd ever seen.

With that Fernando scurried off into the sacristy. He found the trunk still below the window he'd busted out earlier. He stepped up on the trunk and looked out the window. All clear. So he eased himself up on the windowsill and dropped noiselessly to the ground. With his Smith & Wessen in hand he peeked around the corner of the morada. He saw movement in a clump of hollyhocks in the courtyard. The bright red and white flowers on top of the hollyhocks began to sway.

Suddenly Hal appeared between the hollyhocks. Just a glimpse. His shoulder and head.

Just then the shooter behind the bench popped up and fired again, his bullets ricocheting off the adobe wall of the morada just above the open door.

Hank took his time returning fire. Finally he ducked out of the door and fired one shot with his Colt. The bullet exploded the top of the wooden bench shielding the shooter. Tony cursed from behind the bench and fired back.

Hank returned fire again.

Fernando watched Hal moving through the hollyhocks. Then it dawned on him: Hal was trying to move to the far side of the courtyard in order to get a clear shot at Hank when the big man stepped out to fire.

Sure enough, Hal waited until Hank stepped outside and then raised his left arm to shoot.

At that instant Fernando squeezed the trigger of his Smith & Wessen. The bullet struck Hal in the shoulder and exited through his upper back. Hal screamed and crumpled to the ground bringing with him a stand of hollyhock stalks.

Hearing Hal scream, Tony stood up behind the bench. "Hal? What the fuck?"

That was all Hank needed. He fired one shot into the big man's gut.

Tony dropped his weapon and fell, holding his abdomen with both hands.

Hank stepped out of the door and walked slowly toward Tony behind the bench. He stopped when he saw Travis on the porch holding a pistol. "Your game's up, Walker. You're under arrest for the murder of Bill Candelaria."

Travis stood frozen on the porch, seemingly unable to decide what to do. He didn't speak. He didn't shoot. He just stood there.

But Hank wasn't finished. "That ain't all. We know where you keep the drugs, thanks to Belle Longstreet. As soon as we open the trastero in your office, you'll be charged with the possession and sale of illegal drugs. Along with murder. You're gonna be in the big house a long, long time."

"That back-stabbing bitch!" Travis shouted and then ducked quickly into the house.

Meanwhile Fernando came out from behind the morada and walked through the courtyard to Hal, who was writhing in pain. He picked up Hal's handgun and went to join Hank.

Halfway to the patio Fernando saw Tony on the ground reaching for his gun.   "Hank!" Fernando shouted, running toward the house.

Hank pivoted and fired one bullet, striking Tony in the middle of the chest. The big man lay still, flat on his back now.

"Thanks," Hank said to Fernando. "Walker ran into the house."

Just as they reached the patio Fernando heard a vehicle fire up on the far side of the house. The sound took him by surprise. He had no idea there was a road on that side of the property. He ran around the corner of the patio in time to see Travis speeding away on a narrow crushed rock road. The crushed rock looked freshly laid—a recent addition of a secret getaway. Travis was driving the same gray Audi sedan he'd seen in the parking lot earlier.

Fernando listened to the sound of the engine growing fainter.

"Did you get the license number?" Hank asked, coming around the corner to join Fernando.

Fernando held up his hand, still listening. The Audi was traveling east on Highway 64 toward Cimarron.

"He's headed east," Fernando said.

"Well, he won't get far," Hank said. "No doubt he's headed to I-Twenty-five. I'll put out an APB."

Fernando nodded. "I agree. The only way for him to get anywhere fast would be to take I-Twenty-five."

"Yeah, so if he heads north on I-Twenty-five, the Colfax County Sheriff will be waiting for him at Raton," Hank said. "If he heads south on I-Twenty-five, the San Miguel County Sheriff will be waiting at Las Vegas. Just a matter of time at this point."

While Hank called his office Fernando went to check on Roy, who was still sitting inside the door of the morada. He had his eyes closed, leaning back against the adobe wall.

"Hold on, Roy, the ambulance is on its way," Fernando said. "Shouldn't be more than a few minutes now."

Roy opened his eyes and nodded.

Fernando joined Hank on the porch waiting for the ambulance and forensics. The ambulance arrived first with its siren blaring. Once the siren stopped two medics came running down the walkway from the parking lot. The younger of the two carried a stretcher. The older, pot-bellied man in the lead saw them on the porch. "Hey, Hank. What do you have?"

Hank laughed and shook his head. "Afternoon, Jack. What took you so long?"

"The damn traffic," Jack said. "And it's not even summer yet. So what do you have for us?"

"Depends on what you're looking for," Hank said. "We got two injured, two dead, and one on the run."

Jack smiled, a big man with a red face from all the exertion. "Gimme the two injured. I can't help the two dead, and I'm too old and too fat to catch the one on the run."

When the second medic arrived with the stretcher Fernando took them down to the morada. Roy opened his eyes when he saw the medics. "Man am I glad to see you guys," he said.

Fernando pointed to the courtyard. "The other guy's a police hold. He's in the hollyhocks over there. Careful with him, he's a screamer."

The medics carried Roy up to the ambulance and then came back for Hal, who fought them when they loaded him on the stretcher and then screamed all the way to the parking lot.

Forensics arrived a half hour later. They parked their van and came down the walkway with their packs. Hank knew both of them.

"Ricardo! Dean! Got some business for you, one fresh and the other...well, he ain't so fresh."

Ricardo laughed, a tall man with a sculpted body and a thin mustache. "Lead the way, Hank."

Hank motioned to where Tony lay in the dust behind the bench. "There's one. He can wait. Now follow me and I'll show you the other."

Hank led them to the morada. "Watch your step."

Ricardo stopped at the doorway. "Wait. Is this a damn penitente morada? Out here?"

"Used to be," Hank said.

"What's a penitente morada?" Dean asked, a young Anglo. Looked like a teenager. Didn't have a clue.

Hank and Ricardo ignored the question. Hank clicked on the flashlight app on his cell phone and led the two of them through the dark nave back to the sacristy and the sarcophagus.

"That there is Bill Candelaria, the last of the Candelaria family," Hank said solemnly.

Dean took a mask out of his pocket and put it on over his mouth and nose before approaching the sarcophagus.

Ricardo bent over the sarcophagus to get a closer look. "Yeah, I see what you mean. Looks like he's been dead a couple of months." He straightened up and looked at Hank. "Okay, we'll take care of it."

"Much obliged," Hank said.

While they were in the morada Fernando took the opportunity to go off by himself. On the porch he entered the rear door of the house and walked past the shepherd's fireplace and down the long hallway to the room Travis used as an office and bedroom. He stopped when he heard sobbing coming from the kitchen next door. Looking around the corner, he saw Jenny sitting on a bench at the long table with her head in her hands.

"I'm so sorry," she wailed. "I didn't know...really I didn't."

"Are you a nurse?" Fernando asked.

"No, I'm on staff at Taos Valley Nursing Home," she sobbed. "Travis offered me a lot of money to come here and help Dallas."

"Help? What's that supposed to mean?"

"To keep him company and help him with his drugs, what Travis called his therapy," Jenny said. "I knew it was wrong, I did. It's just that we're all so poor...there are no jobs up here, I just...I needed the money. I'm so sorry!"

Fernando couldn't tell if she were acting or genuinely remorseful. "Well, if you testify against Travis, I'm sure the D.A. will cut you a sweet deal. If, that is, you didn't intentionally inject Dallas with the fatal dose."

"Oh God no! I never injected him," she said. "I just brought him the drugs and kept him company...like you saw back at the casita."

Fernando nodded and moved away. He walked into Travis' office next door, hearing Jenny resume her sobbing.

In the office a desk occupied the center of the room, with a single bed along one sidewall and a trastero with hand-carved Zia signs on the other. When he opened the doors of the trastero he found mostly clothes hanging from the rack above and piled in the drawers below. Nothing unusual.

So he shimmied the heavy trastero away from the wall, an inch at a time. Then he took out his knife and went to work prying off the back panel. That turned out to be relatively easy because the panel was loose from being repeatedly removed. When he popped off the false back he found the metal container, a two-foot by three-foot stainless steel box with a lock on top.

While he worked on the trastero he heard Hank and Jenny talking in the kitchen. Hank talking and Jenny wailing. It sounded like she was putting on an equally good show for Hank.

Freeing the metal box, Fernando carried it over to Travis' desk and dropped it on the desktop. He heard Hank's footsteps in the hallway. "You find it?" Hank asked, coming into the office.

"Yeah. It was right where Belle said it would be," Fernando said. He worked at the lock with his pick. It took much longer than it usually did, but he managed to pop it open finally.

"Well, look at that," Hank said, staring at an assortment of bottles and clear bags filled with pills and white powder. "Old Belle Longstreet did us a favor. She saved us a lot of time."

Fernando closed the lid of the box. "What about her," he said, motioning toward the kitchen.

Hank frowned. "Don't worry about Jenny. Dave's on his way from the hospital now. He'll take her in and book her for accessory to murder. She'll plead out and testify against Walker. Like they all do."

"Okay, so let's get out of here," Fernando said, hoisting the metal box.

Hank led the way outside and started up the flagstone path to the parking lot.

Fernando waited until Hank was halfway to the parking lot before shouting "Where you going?"

Hank stopped and turned around.

"We're stuck on the dirt road behind the morada, remember?" Fernando asked.

"Figures," Hank said.

25

"Thanks boys," Hank said to the forensics team.

It had taken Fernando, Dean, and Ricardo only seconds to push the cruiser downhill out of the soft sand where it had been stuck.

"No problem," Dean said. "I don't think our two customers back there mind one bit."

Fernando watched Dean and Ricardo cross over the arroyo to the courtyard. They were working on Tony first. Bill would take more time.

Hank removed his Stetson and wiped the sweat off his face with a kerchief. He turned to Fernando. "So now we wait and let the APB do its business. One of our boys will spot the Audi on I-Twenty-five."

"Waiting's not my strong suit," Fernando said.

'Hah! Me neither!" Hank said. He checked his watch. "You want me to drop you off at the El Pueblo?"

"Sure, but I want you to give me a call as soon as you hear something. Then come pick me up again."

With that, they climbed into Hank's cruiser and followed the dirt road around to where it connected with the driveway. This time they had no trouble crossing the flat arroyo. When they turned on Highway 64 Hank hit the gas and drove like a man possessed. Minutes later they entered Taos. Hank pulled into the El Pueblo parking lot and screeched to a stop in front of Fernando's room.

"Okay, be ready," Hank said. "I'll call you as soon as I hear something. Maybe before!"

"I'll be ready," Fernando said. He stood on his porch a moment watching the cruiser enter traffic on the Paseo and speed off south toward the sheriff's office. Then he opened the door but paused before stepping inside his room.

Fernando hated waiting. Too much time on his hands took him

to the dark side. After thirty years of police work he had too many bad memories, too many things he regretted. Better to stay busy, so he didn't have to think. When the mind wanders, bad stuff happens.

He plopped down in the chair outside his room and looked over the nearly empty parking lot. When someone waved from the office, he waved back begrudgingly and then went inside. He sat in the stuffed chair by the window and checked his email, deleting everything. Then he laid down on the bed and tried to take a nap. That lasted all of fifteen minutes before he climbed out of bed and decided to walk down to the Taos Plaza to pass the time.

Walking by Michael's Kitchen he realized he hadn't eaten anything since early morning, so he stopped in for a quick green chile cheeseburger and then continued on down to the Plaza, where tourists, buskers, and homeless people mingled awkwardly. He sat on a bench and listened to one young man play the guitar and sing Bob Dylan songs. When he got bored with the Bob Dylan wannabe, he walked to the Kit Carson Museum one block down Kit Carson Road. He spent upwards of a boring hour looking at old timey cowboy paraphernalia, reflecting that even a life as memorable as Carson's came down to a few old knick-knacks that nobody in their right mind would want. Depressing as hell. At closing time he and the other visitors were asked to leave, so running out of options he decided to walk down to the Mabel Dodge Luhan House and see if his friend Francis still worked there. He never made it. He'd just left Kit Carson behind when his cell phone rang.

He knew who was calling even before he checked the screen.

"Fernando! We have a sighting!" Hank said. "I'm on my way to pick you up. Be there in five."

"I'm ready," Fernando said, relieved that the wait was over. He wanted to finish this now. No more delays.

He hurried back to his room at the El Pueblo. He had just enough time to use the bathroom and strap on his Smith & Wessen. He was waiting on the porch when Hank drove up in his cruiser.

Hank pulled up next to the Cherokee and stuck his head out of the driver's side window. "Let's roll!"

Fernando jumped into the cruiser. Before he could get the door closed Hank tore out of the parking lot and quickly turned left on Kit Carson Road. Hank stared straight ahead, ignoring Fernando.

"So who called in?" Fernando asked.

"Guy by the name of Benny Alvarez," Hank said. "He's a janitor at the Saint James Hotel in Cimarron. He found the Audi parked behind the hotel dumpsters. That could be a problem."

"What do you mean?"

Hank laughed and turned to Fernando. "Do you know anything about the Saint James?"

Fernando shook his head. "Only that it's old."

"Yeah, well, it's more than old. It's also the most haunted building in the entire Southwest," Hank said. "It was built in the eighteen-seventies on the Old Santa Fe Trail. The list of folks who stayed there reads like a history of the Wild West. I'm talking about Jesse James, Wyatt Earp, Bat Masterson, Billy the Kid, Pat Garrett, Wild Bill Cody, Annie Oakley and just about everyone else coming through on the Trail back in the day. So far there's been at least twenty-six documented murders at the Saint James. You can still see the damn bullet holes in the pressed-tin ceiling of the hotel bar. Thing is, the ghosts of those people who were gunned down there never left the hotel. They're still causing all kinds of hell."

Fernando interrupted Hank's rant. "And how do you know all this?"

"Hah! Personal experience, that's how I know. And reading all the literature they give you at the hotel," Hank said. "I attended a state law enforcement conference there a couple of years ago. I stayed in room thirteen, right next to where Jesse James always stayed in room fourteen. Never slept a wink that night because the damn western posters on the wall started to rattle about midnight and never stopped. Then a light kept turning on and off in the bathroom, but whenever I went to check the light would behave itself. I got so rattled I went down and told the night clerk. He just laughed at me and said, 'welcome to the Saint James.'

"Seems everyone who stays there has the same experience. Some rooms are worse than others. Just down the hall from me was room eighteen, locked up tighter than a banker's ass now because a gunslinger stayed there once and ever since guests have been violently attacked in the room. They gave us a tour of that room the next morning, those of us who were awake enough to see straight There's nothing in there but an old bed frame without a mattress, a rocking chair, and a beat-up old bureau. And on that bureau is a bottle of Jack Daniels and a mess of shot glasses, I kid you not. The guy who gave us the tour said every time they enter the room the booze level in that bottle of Jack Daniels is a little lower. Go figure."

As usual when he listened to ghost stories, Fernando didn't know what to say. Or believe.

"But that ain't even the worst of my experience there," Hank continued. "I was fool enough to take a new recruit with me, a youngster named Jay. He up and disappeared in the middle of the night. Just walked out of his room, as far as we could tell. Next morning we searched for him all over Cimarron and the damn county. Found nothing, not a trace of him. Didn't hear a thing from him for about a week. Then one day Jay wandered into my office looking all disheveled and confused and turned in his badge and gun. He didn't offer any explanation. Just said he no longer wanted to be associated with law enforcement. Thanks but no thanks."

"Did you ever hear from him again?" Fernando asked.

"No, but we heard later he was living up north of Questa in a mountain cabin. "Guess he likes his solitude."

Hank continued to regale him with more history of the Saint James as they drove out of the foothills and entered the grasslands. When he turned off onto State Route 21 into Cimarron, Hank said, "Hope I haven't spooked you."

Fernando laughed. "Nothing spooks me after my experience at Chaco Canyon last year. Tracking down who—or what—murdered Pete Chavez, one of the park rangers there."

"Well, this ain't Chaco Canyon, that's true," Hank said. "Only a couple dozen ghosts at the Saint James, not a couple thousand."

In Cimarron they followed Collision Avenue to the Saint James. The hotel consisted of two massive white buildings, the original adobe building and a newer, more modern building, both rectangular in shape. A spacious patio with blue wrought iron furniture and bright red umbrellas separated the two structures.

Not stopping at the lobby, Hank drove on around behind the hotel toward the Cimarron River. He pointed to a massive dumpster off to the side of the parking lot and pulled over.

"There, you can just see the front fender," Hank said, climbing out of the cruiser and pointing at the dumpster.

Fernando followed, walking around the dumpster to the gray Audi. He smiled when he saw the Texas license plate.

"Yep, he's gonna try to switch cars on us," Hank said.

26

The first thing Fernando noticed when they walked into the lobby of the Saint James was the huge black buffalo head on one wall. He'd never seen a buffalo head on a wall, so he walked over to take a closer look. The animal's short black horns curled up on its head like those he'd seen in caricatures of Satan. Its thick black fur was dusty and mottled and could have dated from the days of Buffalo Bill Cody and the great buffalo hunts of the 1800s.

Hank went directly to the front counter, a dark wooden counter that looked like it belonged in a saloon. Behind the counter an old-fashioned mail and key sorter with dozens of slots took up most of the wall.

"Howdy. Hank Mathews, Taos County Sheriff," Hank said to the nondescript bald man behind the counter. Hank showed the man his badge.

The clerk looked at the badge and then asked, "What can I do for you, sheriff?" He wore a western shirt with a bolo tie. He looked to be in his forties or early fifties but he was as bald as a bowling ball.

Hank took a deep breath. "We're looking for the man who parked his gray Audi behind your dumpster in back. Benny Alvarez called in a tip earlier today. The man is wanted for murder."

The clerk chuckled. "Well, he's come to the right place. We've had more murderers stay here than you can shake a stick at. Some of them were even murdered here. Twenty-six of them, as far as we know."

"So I hear tell," Hank said, not amused. "Travis Walker's his name. He must have checked in mid afternoon. He's about six feet tall, handsome guy with dark hair and a goatee. He was wearing jeans and a white shirt."

The clerk nodded. "Okay, let me look. I just started my shift, so I wouldn't know who checked in this afternoon." He punched a few keys on his computer and shuffled through some papers on the countertop. Then he shook his head. "No, I don't see anyone by that name."

Fernando stepped up to the counter. "In that case he probably used an alias. Look for a single male who checked earlier this afternoon. Can't be many of them, right?"

The clerk nodded again. "Okay, let's see. Yes, it looks like two single males checked in this afternoon. Fred Duda in Room eleven and Mike Banks in Room seventeen."

"Much obliged," Fernando said.

"Maybe one of them's the murderer, you think?" the clerk asked, eager to help. "Who'd he murder?"

Hank smiled, ignoring the question. "Good enough. One more thing. Do you know what a chop shop is?"

"For stolen automobiles? Sure."

"So are there any chop shops or used car lots in Cimarron where a man could swap his car fast?" Hank asked.

The clerk laughed at this. "Chop shop? Cimarron's lucky to have a gas station. We're about as tiny as you can get and still call yourself a town. You'd have to go all the way to Raton for something like that. Why do you ask?"

"Because I expect Walker is trying to ditch his car," Hank said. "He gets on I-Twenty-five in his gray Audi he's a dead man. I got the highway patrol and county sheriffs from Raton to Albuquerque looking for him."

"Makes sense," the clerk said, "but I don't know where he'd get another car around here."

Hank stepped away from the counter and waved at Fernando to follow "Take a look at this place before we go up. It's one of a kind."

They walked through a short hallway into the saloon, a dimly lit room with dark wood paneling and a pressed tin ceiling. Hank stopped under a chandelier and pointed up at the tin ceiling. "You see the bullet holes?"

Fernando saw them. More than he could count.

They did a quick tour of the first floor. All the rooms had pressed tin ceilings, brick fireplaces painted white, and mangy animal heads hanging on the walls: deer, antelope, elk, and several more buffalo heads as big and black as the one in the lobby. Also hanging on the walls were dozens of old photographs and black and white drawings of the famous men and women who had stayed at the Saint James, including those who had been murdered or done the murdering. The rooms contained displays of firearms, spurs, saddles and other cowboy gear. Everything was right out of the Wild West of the 1800s.

When they finished their walk-through they came back to the lobby and the wooden stairway leading to the second floor.

"Ready?" Hank asked.

"You first, you're the lawman," Fernando said.

"Okay, let's take the rooms in order. Fred or Mike, one of them's gotta be Walker."

Fernando let Hank lead the way up the creaky stairway and then followed at a safe distance. He didn't want to make it easy for a shooter, if Travis was a shooter. He had no idea how dangerous Travis might be.

The wooden steps creaked and moaned plaintively as they tip-toed up the stairs. At the top they stopped to listen. The long hallway looked dark and forlorn in the half-light of dusk, the only light coming from a chandelier in the center of the hallway and a small window at the far end of the building. A ratty antelope's head glared at them from the wall. Not a sound anywhere in the hotel. It felt like they were in a mausoleum for dead, stuffed animals.

They crept along the dark hallway under the nose of the antelope until they came to Room 11. Hank removed his Colt from its holster and with his other hand knocked lightly on the door with his knuckles.

Fernando readied his Smith & Wessen.

They heard a shuffling sound from inside the room. Then a light cough, followed by a wheezing sound. Someone inside was having difficulty breathing. Didn't sound like Travis.

When the door opened, they found themselves looking at a shrunken asthmatic old man wearing carpenter jeans and red suspenders over yellowed long underwear. He had a days-old beard and a few tufts of gray hair sticking up in various directions on his head and in his ears.

"Howdy," the old timer said, his eyes bright with enthusiasm. "Are you all doin' a reenactment for the hotel? I like your black hat. It looks authentic, for sure."

Hank stepped back. "What?"

"Name's Fred Duda. I'm from up near Plum Creek in the Nebraska panhandle," the old man said cheerfully. "I'm on the trail of the notorious Billy the Kid. He stayed in this room, you know. At least that's what they said downstairs when they gave me the room. I think."

Fred paused to get his breath. "Yeah, this was my first stop. Tomorrow I'm headed down to Lincoln County to see the jail where Billy was held. You know, where he escaped and killed the lawman."

"I beg your pardon?" Hank said, and showed the man his badge.

"Oh, sorry, I don't have nothin' against lawmen," Fred said, wheezing. "I'm just a big fan of Billy's. Look at all the books I been reading about Billy and Pat Garrett." He took them over to a small end table beside the brass bed and showed them his collection of Billy the Kid books.

Hank turned to Fernando.

Fernando shrugged and said, "Okay, enjoy your stay and your trip to Lincoln. You'll love it down there."

"I know!" Fred said enthusiastically. "You boys take care, now."

Fernando closed the door behind him. Hank was already moving quietly down the hall, reading the numbers on the doors. When he came to Room 17 he stopped and waited for Fernando.

They moved to either side of the door, guns in hand. Then Hank tapped lightly on the door with his knuckles. They heard rummaging inside.

Hank tapped on the door again. "Travis, come out with your hands up. We know you're in there."

Silence.

"Do yourself a favor, Travis," Hank continued. "Come out now and we'll see what we can do to help you with the District Attorney. Maybe he'll cut you some slack. He's a reasonable guy."

Without warning Travis fired two shots from inside the room.

POP! POP!

The door splintered in front of them as the bullets ripped through the wood and showered them with fragments.

Suddenly the chandelier light in the hallway flashed on and off. The house seemed to groan as the wind howled outside the hotel.

"Cover me," Hank said, standing back a pace. He raised his right leg and with his boot kicked the flimsy door wide open. The door slammed back into the wall, rattling the hallway. Then Hank moved into the room holding his Colt in front of him with both hands.

Fernando ducked down and glanced around the corner of the door, seeing an empty room that looked exactly like Fred's. No Travis. The wide open balcony doors swung back and forth in the wind. Travis had either climbed down or jumped from the second floor balcony.

"Shit!" Hank cursed, rushing out on the balcony.

Fernando followed Hank into the room. He took a step forward and suddenly stopped. In the mirror on the wall he saw someone standing behind him, a tall man dressed all in black with a black bushy mustache. He spun around, Smith & Wessen in hand, but there was no one there to see. The man in black had disappeared. Spooked, he turned to the balcony.

POP! Outside another round hit the balcony door.

Hank hit the deck and returned fire.

Crouching, Fernando eased out on the opposite side of the balcony. From his perch near the railing he watched Travis fire off one more round, which ricocheted off the side of the hotel. Then Travis ran through the parking lot and ducked behind the hotel. They would never catch him before he reached his Audi.

"Let's go!" Hank said, picking himself up and crashing through the balcony doors.

They ran out of the room and down the hallway past the head of the dead antelope. On the rickety wooden stairway the two of them sounded like a herd of stampeding steers.

In the lobby Fernando saw the clerk's head pop up over the counter. The clerk had ducked under the counter for safety.

"Are you guys okay?" the clerk asked. "What's going on up there? I heard gunshots."

"Our man jumped off the balcony and got away," Fernando said, trying to catch up with Hank who'd already run out to the parking lot.

Hank had the cruiser running and ready to roll when Fernando climbed into the passenger's seat. He backed the cruiser out of its parking space and took off fast, cutting through a vacant lot to State Route 21. The cruiser's tires slid across loose dirt and gravel in the ditch and then caught on the pavement. They raced up the narrow lane toward the highway.

Hank pointed to the intersection in the distance. They saw the gray Audi turning left on Highway 64 heading back toward Taos.

"Where the hell is he going now?" Fernando asked.

27

By the time they reached Highway 64 the Audi was nowhere in sight. They knew the cruiser would never be able to keep up with the speedy Audi. So Hank pulled over on the side of the highway and called his office for backup. He asked the dispatcher to send a unit just outside the eastern city limits to apprehend Walker before he could enter the city and endanger innocent bystanders. He explained it as an effort to minimize collateral damage.

To the west the sun had already disappeared behind the majestic Taos mountains, leaving streaks of crimson and purple hovering over the highest peaks. The ranchland on both sides of the highway was lost in deepening shadows. Fernando figured they had at most an hour of daylight left, if you could call dusk in a mountain terrain daylight. Not a lot of time to track down someone driving a vehicle as fast as an Audi.

When Hank finished his call he hit the ignition and steered the unwieldy cruiser back onto the highway. He gunned the engine and took off fast over the uneven pavement.

When the speedometer hit 90 mph, Fernando glanced at Hank. The big man stared straight ahead, both hands fixed on the steering wheel.

"You might slow down...just so we can actually see something other than a blur," Fernando said.

"Hah! Very funny."

Approaching the foothills Hank slowed down for the curves. Shadows seem to come out of the foothills to meet them.

Suddenly Hank slammed on the brakes. The cruiser fishtailed and slid sideways onto the shoulder of the highway, nearly rolling over.

"Whoa!" Fernando said as his body lashed against the door. Only his seatbelt kept him from flying out the open window. "Slow the fuck down, will you!"

Hank pointed to the north side of the highway. "Over there by that old gray house. Isn't that Travis' Audi?"

Fernando looked to where Hank pointed. He, too, saw the Audi. What surprised him more was that it was parked in front of Jerry and Clyde's ramshackle house. Why would Travis stop there? He'd already fired Jerry.

"That's where the groundskeeper at the ranch lives," Fernando said. "You remember Jerry, the skinny guy with red hair who passed me the note? I followed him here the other day to ask about Travis."

Hank whistled. "I don't like the looks of this, no sir," Hank said. He turned the cruiser around and drove slowly back to the driveway, where he stopped and switched off the engine. They sat there for a few minutes in silence.

"You think it's an ambush?" Hank asked.

Fernando shook his head. "No. If it is, it's just Travis. I doubt Jerry's going to help him."

"Why not?"

"Well, for one thing, Travis fired him," Fernando said. "And for another Jerry was fond of Bill Candelaria, who Travis murdered. Plus, Jerry doesn't strike me as the violent type. That's my read."

"Okay, let's do it," Hank said, and started the engine. He drove slowly down the long drive toward the gray, unpainted house with the wraparound porch and the sagging gables.

Coming closer they saw some sort of commotion in the yard.

"I forgot to tell you, watch out for the deranged old man with a shotgun," Fernando warned.

"Who the hell is that?"

"Jerry's father, Clyde." Fernando said. "He's in a wheelchair but he's suspicious of outsiders and meaner than a rattlesnake."

"Great," Hank said.

As they approached, the scene before them continued to unfold. The Audi had come to a stop behind Jerry's old Ford pickup. Travis lay in the dirt near the Audi struggling to get to his hands and knees and reaching for the open door of the Audi. Up on the porch Clyde sat in his wheelchair yelling and waving his shotgun at Travis. Between the two Jerry jumped up and down hysterically in the driveway shouting at his father.

Fernando had no idea what had happened. Had the old man started shooting? Why else would Travis be on the ground?

When Jerry saw the cruiser approaching he ran out to meet them. "Help! Help!" he screamed.

Hank rolled down his window. "What's going on here?"

"Mr. Walker wanted to trade his Audi for our pickup and my father shot him," Jerry said, out of breath. "I don't know how to stop him. I'm afraid he's gonna kill Mr. Walker."

Hank pulled up behind the Audi and set the brake.

Not waiting, Fernando jumped out of the cruiser and ran over to Travis, who seemed to be in shock. The back of Travis' white shirt had been shredded by buckshot. Red circles pockmarked the shirt, oozing blood.

"Can you get up?" Fernando asked. When he tried to help him up Travis moaned in pain and pulled away.

Instead Travis managed to crawl over to the Audi and sit up, leaning back against the front fender. His eyes stared straight ahead.

Fernando turned to the porch and shouted at the old man. "Don't shoot, you crazy bastard! Put the gun away!"

At that point Hank took charge. He stepped up to the porch holding his Colt and said, "Mister, I'm the county sheriff and you're gonna be in a whole lot of trouble unless you drop that shotgun. You hear me?"

"Hah! I don't give a damn about the law. Whatcha gonna do, arrest me? I'm just protecting my property."

"Drop the gun, old man."

Clyde pointed to Travis. "He tried to steal my truck, goddamnit! Why don't you arrest him?"

Hank pointed the gun at the old man's chest. "He's already under arrest. Now drop the gun."

While the two men argued Fernando snuck around the Audi and then the Ford to the corner of the house. He climbed over the porch railing and crept up behind the wheelchair. He managed to get within ten feet before the old man heard him and turned his head.

"Why, you—" Clyde muttered and tried to swing around the heavy shotgun. Before he could Fernando rushed over and grabbed the barrel of the shotgun. But the old man fought like a tiger, surprisingly strong for his age. The two of them wrestled with the shotgun before Fernando managed to gain control. Finally he yanked it out of the old man's hands.

"No!" the old man shouted and lunged for the shotgun, but Fernando managed to push him away.

"Okay, calm down now!" Fernando shouted. "I don't want to hurt you, goddamnit!"

"Get offa me, you sonofabitch!" Clyde screamed and then pulled a hunting knife off his belt. He swung wildly at Fernando.

"You want me to shoot him?" Hank asked from across the way. He waved his Colt.

"No, he'll calm down. One way or another."

"Like hell I will," the old man said and wheeled his chair around ferociously and again swung the knife at Fernando.

Now Fernando was pissed. He swung the shotgun in a wide arc, smashing the old man's outreached hand and sending the knife flying off the porch. Then he kicked the wheelchair to push it away from him.

The old man stared at Fernando for a moment and then at Hank. "Well, fuck you both," he said, and then turned and wheeled back into the house.

Now that he didn't have to deal with the old man, Fernando joined Hank at the Audi, tending to Travis.

"Like I said, you're under arrest for murder and for the possession and sale of illegal drugs," Hank said to Travis and then read him his Miranda Rights. "Can you walk?"

Travis moaned and shook his head.

"Well, the buckshot's not gonna kill you, but it'll hurt like hell until we get you to an ER."

Travis moaned again.

Hank turned to Fernando. "Keep the peace while I call for another ambulance. Won't they be happy?"

Jerry joined Fernando while Hank went to make his call. "I'm really sorry about all this," Jerry said. "My father doesn't mean any harm. He's just a grumpy old man. He thought Mister Walker was here to steal our truck. I think he might be getting some dementia, you know? He keeps forgetting things and getting mad at me when I try to help him."

Fernando nodded. "I do. I've seen it in my own family. By the way, thanks for the tip about the dump and Bill Candelaria's car. Did you know they killed Candelaria and put his body in the morada?"

Jerry lowered his head. "I suspected Mr. Candelaria was dead when they asked me to drive the car into the dump. I shouldn't a done it, I suppose. I knew something was wrong."

While they talked Hank came back. "Okay, the ambulance is on its way. Should be here in twenty minutes. Same pair."

"So what do you want to do with the shotgun?" Fernando asked, holding up the gun.

Hank turned to Jerry. "Can you hide it somewhere? To keep it away from your dad?"

"Oh, I don't know," Jerry said. "He loves that old four ten. That used to be my gun when I was a teenager and we went bird hunting."

Hank nodded. "I understand, but it's dangerous letting the old boy have a loaded weapon. Tell you what. Let him have the gun, but hide the shells. If he gets suspicious, just put an empty shell or two in the chamber.

He won't know the difference. Years back I had an uncle with Alzheimer's who used to shoot up his farm and we did just that. Worked like magic."

Jerry seemed to like that idea. "I'll give it a try."

When the ambulance arrived, the two medics jumped out of the ambulance and rushed over with a stretcher and their gear. The pot-belied older man laughed. "How many more of these are you going to have for me today? They're piling up in the emergency room."

"One of those days," Hank said.

While the two medics tended to Travis, Hank called his station and explained the situation. He told the dispatcher to send one of the newer cops to Holy Cross Hospital. "Put Walker on a twenty-four hour watch until he can be transported to jail. Same for the other guy I called in earlier. Maybe the two of them can share a room so we'll only have to send one cop to the hospital. Okay?"

Travis howled with pain when the medics put him on the stretcher. He begged for something to cut the pain but the medics ignored him. Instead they lifted the stretcher and carried him to the ambulance.

Fernando and Hank watched the ambulance drive down to Highway 64 and turn right toward Taos.

Fernando handed the shotgun to Jerry. "I need to get back to Santa Fe."

"I'll drop you off at the El Pueblo," Hank said, checking his watch. "Yep, they're gonna charge you for the night. Even if you don't stay."

28

Fernando pulled into the parking lot in front of his office well after sunset. The streetlights bathed Canyon Road in a soft yellow glow. A few tourists still walked up and down Canyon Road, looking for restaurants or galleries that were still open. He parked the Cherokee in his usual spot and walked down the path to his office. Given the lateness of the hour he didn't bother to change the window sign from closed to open. Instead he switched on the lights and made a beeline to his mini-refrigerator. His plan was to keep a supply water and Modelo, but lately he'd been drinking more Modelo than water. He checked the refrigerator and then helped himself to one of the two remaining bottles of Modelo. If ever he needed a drink, it was now.

Sitting at his desk he found two messages on the machine. The first was from none other than Al, Belle Longstreet's driver, consisting of a succinct five-word statement: "You're a dead man, Lopez."

The second turned out to be from Oralia Ortiz, Danny's wife. Yet another twinge of guilt and remorse came over him as he listened to her sad, resigned voice: "Mister Lopez, this is Oralia Ortiz. I wanted to let you know that I don't have the money to pay you. I'm struggling right now with Danny gone and a baby on the way. Times are hard, you know. I can't pay my bills or nothing. And I don't really care anymore who killed Danny. Doesn't matter anymore. I mean, he's gone, so what difference does it make who killed him?"

What difference indeed? Not even the police cared. So why did he feel such remorse?

Fernando opened the top drawer of his desk and found her retainer check, which he tore in half and tucked into his shirt pocket. Under the circumstances he couldn't accept her money. Just didn't seem right.

He took out his ledger book and scanned the numbers. Since opening earlier in the year he'd barely covered his expenses. He was fast becoming a private investigator *pro bono*.

With that sobering thought he finished his Modelo and thought about heading home. He had to face the music with Estelle sooner or later, so why keep putting it off? He put everything away and locked up for the night. Stepping outside he smelled the fresh Alpine air, cool now that the heat of the day had all but dissipated. From his porch he saw a line of cars driving by on Alameda Street below, heading toward downtown. He walked up to the parking lot into the yellow glow of the streetlights that held back the dark night.

He noticed a nondescript sedan parked across the street in the shadows. What made it suspicious was that it blocked the driveway of the gallery across the street, which looked closed for the night. He didn't remember seeing this particular vehicle before in his Canyon Road neighborhood, so he figured it must be a rental. Keeping an eye on the sedan, he walked over to his Cherokee and reached for the door handle. Just then he saw a one-arm man step out of the shadows near the sedan and walk across Canyon Road into the light.

"Not so fast, Lopez!" the man said.

Fernando spun around, feeling a surge of adrenaline when he noticed a sling on the man's right arm and recognized his attacker. Larry held a gun in his left hand. Looked like a Glock, semi-automatic. A nasty weapon.

Fernando quickly scanned the lay of the land: Ruby's porch and gallery to his left—Essentia's short adobe wall to his right. Not much to work with, but it would have to do.

He took his Smith & Wessen out of its holster and stepped away from the Cherokee. The last thing he wanted was more bullet holes in his Cherokee. He had enough of them already.

"What do you want, Larry?" Fernando asked.

"What do I want? I'm the Grim Reaper. I've come to collect."

"Don't be stupid. Get out of here while you still can," Fernando said.

Larry grinned and continued to advance. When he reached the edge of the parking lot he opened fire: POP! POP! POP!

The bullets clipped through the leaves of the cottonwoods behind Fernando or thudded into the gravel of the parking lot.

Then Fernando remembered that Larry was right-handed—the hand in the sling. Evidently he couldn't shoot worth a damn with his left hand. "Put your gun away, Larry, before I have to shoot you," he shouted.

"Fuck you!" Larry responded.

Then Larry ran toward Ruby's porch. While running he fired off a couple of wild shots, his bullets ricocheting off the adobe wall in front of Essentia.

Fernando smiled. It was like watching a fat man with a sling on his arm playing Butch Cassidy and the Sundance Kid.

Larry stopped to change clips. Then he darted into the shadow of Fernando's 'Private Eye' sign.

Fernando moved down toward Essentia, taking cover behind the adobe wall. If Butch Cassidy came after him, fat Butch would be totally exposed.

POP! POP! POP! Larry fired wildly as he lumbered down the hill toward Essentia. A damn fool.

"Last warning, Larry!" Fernando shouted. "Put your gun away and get the hell out of here or I'm gonna have to shoot you."

"Fuck you!" Larry shouted again.

Fernando debated whether to shoot the sonofabitch and be done with him once and for all but decided against it. If he did he would be spending another two or three hours here explaining the situation to the Santa Fe Police Department. They didn't do anything fast. Plus the convoluted tale he would be forced to tell would involve a lot of unsavory people and raise a host of unpleasant questions, all of which would tie him up for weeks, if not months.

So instead Fernando waited until Larry was halfway to Essentia and totally exposed. Then he took aim at the Glock in Larry's outstretched hand and squeezed the trigger. The bullet zinged off the metal gun, sending the Glock flying through the air. Larry screamed and started waving his hand up and down, as though he were trying to shake off the hurt. Then he rubbed his hand on his pants and sank to his knees cursing. "You motherfucker! You motherfucker!" he repeated.

Behind Fernando the door to Essentia opened slightly and the owners, Paul and June Bryan, peeked out on the mayhem. "Who's there?" Paul asked.

"It's me, Fernando. Don't worry. Everything's under control."

The Bryans opened the door wider and stared, still wary.

Fernando walked out from behind the wall and over to Larry, who was trying to free his right hand from the sling in order to tend to his bloody left hand. Trying to staunch the bleeding.

"Goddamnit, Larry, why can't you just get the hell out of town like the rest of them?" Fernando asked. They're all going back to Austin. Why can't you? Just fucking disappear!"

Larry growled to himself.

Fernando heard footsteps behind him.

"Can I help?" June asked. "His hand's bleeding."

"Yeah. Keep an eye on him while I get my first aid kit," Fernando said. "If he gives you any trouble, kick him in the crotch."

Fernando walked to his Cherokee and opened the rear hatch. He searched through the assortment of supplies he kept in the back compartment looking for his first aid kit. Then he remembered he'd moved the first aid kit into his office when he cut his hand last week. So he went into his office and found the kit on a shelf in the closet. When he returned Larry was sitting up on a bench out front of Essentia and June was examining his bleeding hand.

"Here, let me get in there," Fernando said. He first poured hydrogen peroxide over Larry's hand and then wound a cloth bandage around his hand and through his fingers. Then he taped the bandage with medical tape.

"Not bad," June said, looking at Fernando's work. She waved and went back inside Essentia.

Larry shook his head, still angry. "How the fuck am I supposed to drive with two bad hands?"

"Use your thumb," Fernando said. "Whatever it takes."

Larry turned away.

"Why the hell didn't you leave town?" Fernando asked again. "You had the opportunity. Did you really have to stick around to kill someone else, like you killed Danny."

"Wait a minute, I didn't kill Danny!" Larry shot back.

"What about the torn check Paula found it your waste basket?"

"Scott dropped it there," Larry said. "Scott didn't have a desk with a waste basket in his room, so he used mine. The basket was inside the door to my room. Right off the hallway."

"What are you saying? That Scott killed Danny?"

"Of course he killed Danny!" Larry said. "He snapped. When I knocked Danny down, Scott jumped on him and wouldn't let go. We were just supposed to get the check, but the fucker went crazy. He choked Danny to death. I tried to stop him but it was too late."

Fernando remained skeptical. "Scott's a wimp. He doesn't seem like the murdering type. Like you."

"Yeah, well, fuck you, Lopez! I'm telling you the truth. He snapped, he went crazy, that's what happened.

Fernando considered. "I'll tell you what. If you leave tonight, get the hell out of town and don't come back, I won't call the police. I'll let this drop. No harm, no foul. What do you say?"

"Sure," Larry said. "I hate this fucking town anyway. Just a bunch of rich fucks. I'll be glad to get back to Texas."

"You do that," Fernando said. "If you come here again, I won't aim for your hand. You understand? I'll shoot you right between the eyes."

Larry glared at him for a moment and then got awkwardly to his feet. He grimaced whenever he had to use his left hand. After he managed to get his balance he hobbled down to his sedan and drove off,

Smiling, Fernando watched the sedan disappear up Canyon Road, weaving from one side of the road to the other.

29

Feeling too agitated to go home, Fernando went back into his office and opened his last can of Modelo. He made a mental note to stop by the IGA for more beer tomorrow. What Larry had said about Danny's murder further muddled the situation. Not that he trusted Larry, he didn't. But neither did he trust Scott, who was as slick as they come, a real salesman. His performance at the La Fonda bar claiming Larry had killed Danny could have won an Academy Award. And he trusted Belle least of all. She was the mastermind, the puppeteer behind everything that had happened in this sordid affair. She'd set up Danny and Dallas and Travis. He saw it clearly now. She'd played all of them to get what she wanted and even tried to play him.

The more Fernando brooded, the more enraged he became. He hated to be played. Hated it so much that, mad as hell, he locked up his office and jumped into the Cherokee. He raced around the Paseo, so worked up that he forgot to turn on his headlights until he turned onto Bishop's Lodge Road and sped down the dark hill toward Tesuque. It had been a long, exhausting day but he desperately wanted closure. He wanted to finish this nasty business and be rid of the whole lot of them.

At the entrance to Bishop's Lodge Resort he slowed down and drove quietly around the outer road to Cottonwood Casita. As before he parked behind the casita, dark now except for a faint light in one of the back bedroom windows. He slid out of the Cherokee, opening and closing the door quietly. He wanted to keep the element of surprise. He didn't want to give Belle time to devise a plan to lie her way out of taking responsibility for the death and destruction she had caused.

He walked gingerly around the flower garden to the front door and took out his lock pick. It turned out the pick wasn't necessary. Belle hadn't even bothered to lock the door.

Fernando opened the door and stepped into the dark casita. He crept slowly toward the light coming from under the partially closed door of the master bedroom. A burst of adrenaline fueled his anger.

Approaching the door he heard Belle moan inside the bedroom.

With one motion he kicked open the door, which slammed against the wall sending paint and plaster flying through the air. The deafening noise rattled the casita. Belle shrieked.

Fernando smiled at what he saw: Belle and Scott naked in bed fucking. Belle on top, with Scott lying passively underneath.

"How...dare you!" she sputtered, dis-engorging herself from Scott. She jumped out of bed and pulled a sheet around her full, padded body. Left naked on the bed, Scott grabbed a pillow to cover his private parts.

"So you like your playthings young, eh," Fernando said, still smiling. It wasn't a question.

"That's none of your business!" She spit her words at him, angry and flustered and barely able to speak. "What do you want?"

Fernando answered her question with a heavy dose of sarcasm. "To congratulate you! You got what you wanted. You won. You got it all, just like you planned. Even if you had to eliminate a few people along the way, including Danny and your husband and now Travis. You knocked them off one after another. Amazing work."

"I don't know what you're talking about," Belle shot back. "I never killed anyone."

"Not by yourself," Fernando said. "You would never stoop so low to get your hands dirty. You made other people do your dirty work. Your boy toy here lost his cool and killed Danny."

Suddenly Scott stirred in the bedroom. "You can't prove that." He crawled out of bed and grabbed his underwear and jeans and quickly put them on.

"And you drove the getaway car," Fernando continued. "That was your contribution."

Belle stared at him with hatred in her eyes.

Fernando stared back. "Up at the ranch in Taos Jenny and Travis killed your husband for you," he said. "And then Travis had to go because he knew too much, so you turned on him and gave him up to the sheriff's office. He's facing years in a Federal prison while you go scot-free and end up with all the money. Dallas' money mostly, although I suppose you have your own trust account. People like you usually do. But they always want more."

"Let me tell you something," Belle said, walking out of the bedroom into the living area. "Danny was a lowlife, a no account musician who lived off my husband. My Husband was a reckless, undisciplined drunk and drug addict. And as for Travis, he's a cheap con-man, a grifter. He stole from my husband—and me—for years. They all deserved what they got."

"And you're nothing but a cheap, high-rent hooker," Fernando said. "So what do you deserve?"

Furious, Belle took a step forward. For a moment Fernando thought she might lash out at him. That would be a big mistake. But at the last instant she caught herself and stopped.

"You don't know anything about me," Belle said. "You're just a two-bit detective from a two-bit city."

"Private investigator," Fernando corrected her. "But you didn't answer my question. What do you deserve?"

"I deserve to be free of all you lowlifes, you and the rest of them."

"So that's how you justify what you did?" Fernando asked. "It's that easy for you to sign someone's death warrant because you think he's nothing but a lowlife? And then walk away?"

"Oh, go to hell! Who are you to judge someone like me? Who cares what you think anyway?"

"You do, because I have enough evidence to put you and your boy toy here away for a long time," Fernando said, taking some liberties with the facts. "What do you think I was doing in Taos all week?"

Fernando smiled, watching Belle squirm. "What do you mean?" she asked.

"Just that," he said. "I know what you and Travis and Jenny did. Everything about your plan."

She stared at him for a long moment. "So what do you want?"

"I want you to write a check to Oralia Ortiz, Danny's wife," Fernando said. "You took away her only means of support when you had Danny killed. She's pregnant and in desperate straits."

She sneered at him. "So you're going to hit me up for money too, just like all the others."

"No, I wouldn't touch a penny of your dirty money," he said. "What I want is for you to help Oralia."

Scott again intervened. "Don't listen to him, Belle. He's bluffing. Let me take care of him."

"Try me," Fernando said.

Scott puffed up his bare chest and came raging into the living area. "Get out before I throw you out!"

Fernando smiled, standing his ground.

"Now!" Scott shouted and lashed out with his right hand.

The glancing blow grazed Fernando's chin as he ducked to his left. He took a half step forward and then drove his right hand into Scott's midsection as hard as he could. Twice.

Scott doubled over, gasping for air. He staggered back and then looked wildly around for something he could use as a weapon. He spotted the iron poker at the fireplace and stumbled across the room to grab it. Turning around, he raised the iron poker and walked unsteadily toward Fernando.

Fernando sighed. He calmly pulled out his Smith & Wessen and pointed it at Scott's head. "Put it down, lover boy, or I'll give you a third eye right in the center of your forehead."

"Scott! Put it down!" Belle screamed.

Scott stared at Belle for a moment and then reluctantly dropped the poker. The metal poker clanked on the tile floor. Scott took a seat on the sofa, still trying to get his breath. He shook his head.

Belle frowned at Scott and then turned to Fernando. With a pained expression on her face she asked, "How much do you want?"

"One hundred thousand. That ought to cover her living expenses for a while."

"One hundred?" Belle pretended to be shocked.

"Come on, Belle, a hundred thousand is nothing to you," Fernando said. It's spare change. You'll spend at least that on your pretty boy here before you leave Bishop's Lodge."

"I'll give her seventy-five thousand, not a penny more," she said.

Fernando shrugged. "Then make it out to Fernando Lopez and write 'For Oralia Ortiz' on the memo line. That way I can cash it at my bank tomorrow morning and then give the cash to Oralia. If you try to cancel the check, I'll go right to the Sheriff's office in Taos."

She turned abruptly and stomped across the living room floor to a roll-top desk and opened the top. Without sitting, she took her checkbook out of a small drawer and wrote the check. Then she stomped across the floor to where he was standing and handed him the check. "Now get the fuck out of here," she snarled, dropping her aristocratic demeanor.

Fernando examined the check and then tucked it in his shirt pocket. "Sure, but let me ask you one more question. Did you enjoy killing Bill Candelaria, the owner of the ranch in Taos and the last of the family that had owned the property for two hundred years? He was an old man, the last of his line. Were you there when Travis had him killed?"

"You're a sonofabitch, aren't you?" Belle said.

Fernando smiled. "Just doing my job, lady."

Belle and Scott watched him walk out of the Cottonwood Casita. He closed the door quietly behind him and headed home. It had been the longest day he could ever remember.

30

On the way to his office next morning Fernando stopped at the bank and cashed Belle's check. With the cash he purchased a cashier's check made out to Oralia Ortiz for seventy-five thousand dollars. He considered keeping a couple thousand to cover his expenses but decided against it. Oralia needed the money a lot more than he did. *Pro bono.* What could he say?

He took the Paseo around to Otero Street and climbed the hill to Oralia's duplex. The cinderblock building with the rusted tin roof looked even worse in broad daylight. He parked at the end of the drive and walked up the broken concrete. The front yard consisted of dirt with a few weeds growing along the drive. The For Rent sign for the vacant half of the duplex exhibited a few bullet holes he hadn't noticed on his last visit. Were they new?

Fernando walked up to the slab concrete porch and knocked on the door. No answer, so he knocked again. He listened but heard no movement or voices inside. Oralia must have left for work at Ruby's pottery co-op. Like Ruby, Oralia threw pots and created ceramic light fixtures, as well as the occasional sculpture, which she sold in Ruby's gallery next door to his office. For a moment he considered driving down to the co-op in the Railyard District. In the end he decided against it. Better to meet with her privately.

So he climbed back into his Cherokee and followed the Paseo to Canyon Road. Tourists were just beginning to congregate on the streets and sidewalks of the historic street. He pulled into his parking lot and gave directions to an elderly couple who asked where the glass blowing factory was located. Then he quickly retreated to his office, away from the tourists.

Once inside, he turned the sign on his window from Closed to Open and sat down at his desk. There were no messages on the machine so he phoned Oralia right away.

"Yes...?" she answered.

"Oralia, this is Fernando Lopez," he said. "I apologize for not calling sooner. I got involved in other matters and wasn't able to get back to you. It's a long story. Too long to explain over the phone."

Oralia was silent for a moment and then asked, "Did you get my message? I don't have the money to pay you."

"That's what I'm calling about," Fernando said. "Don't worry about the bill. In fact, I'm not going to cash your retainer check. I tossed it."

"Oh, well thank you," she said.

"Listen, I have something important for you here," Fernando said. "Can you come to my office?"

"Okay. I guess I could drive up on my lunch hour, say eleven thirty?"

"See you at eleven thirty then," he said.

While he waited Fernando went next door to Ruby's gallery and had a cup of coffee with Ruby. She'd read about Dallas Longstreet's death and wanted to know the details, so he gave her the long roundabout version, including the intrigue at both Bishop's Lodge Resort and Painted Skull Ranch. He told her about Belle's machinations, her attempts to eliminate first Danny and then Dallas, her husband. Then he got carried away and also told her about finding Bill Candelaria's body in the morada and the illegal drugs Travis Walker was selling at Painted Skull Ranch. And he told her about chasing Travis to the Saint James Hotel in Cimarron and then capturing him at a ranch where he was attempting to ditch his car.

"Whoa, wait a minute," Ruby said, shaking her head. "Go back. What about Dallas? Did he overdose or not?"

Fernando shook his head. "The medical investigator hasn't ruled yet. But even if he did, the overdose was provided, if not administered, by Travis Walker and his hired hands."

"To get rid of Dallas," Ruby said. "So Belle would get his money."

"Exactly," Fernando said. "Then she turned in Travis to get rid of him. That was her plan all along. Danny Ortiz was just collateral damage."

"So she's what they call a black widow. Jesus!" Ruby laughed. "What a twisted tale."

A few minutes later, when Ruby got busy with a group of tourists who wandered in off Canyon Road, he went back to his office and waited. Right on time he heard a car pull into his gravel parking lot. Moments later Oralia appeared outside his door. He recognized her moon face and long black hair immediately. He hurried over to open the door for her.

"Come in," he said, holding the door open for her.

"Thanks." She walked slowly to the chair, clutching her stomach with both hands as before.

"When's the baby due?" he asked.

"Next month," she said, laughing. "If I can make it that long."

"Do you have help? I mean now that Danny's not there."

"Yes, my mother's coming down from Durango," she said. "And my friends have been great. You saw them the other night. They'll probably be more help than Danny would have been."

"Good," he said, sitting at his desk. He took the cashier's check out of his shirt pocket and handed it to her. "And I hope this helps. At least gets you through this tough period."

Oralia looked at the check, clearly stunned. "What's this? I don't understand. Where did this come from?" She laughed. "I'm supposed to pay you, not the other way around."

"From Belle Longstreet. She wanted to help you out," Fernando said, stretching the truth a bit.

"I can't believe it! This is amazing! Thank her for me, please!"

"I will, if I see her," he said.

Oralia continued to stare at the check.

"I also wanted to give you an update on my investigation," he said. "I don't want you to think I did nothing for the past week."

She shook her head. "Not at all."

"I don't know for sure who killed Danny," Fernando said. "Here's what happened. Dallas gave Danny a check before he left for Taos. Belle found out and sent two guys who work for her to take back the check from Danny. The two guys, Larry and Scott, ambushed Danny in Cathedral Park Saturday night. Things got out of hand and they ended up killing Danny. Larry blames Scott and Scott blames Larry. Truth is, both men were involved in the killing."

"Belle sent them?" she asked.

"Yes, not only sent them, Belle drove the getaway car," Fernando said. "She was divorcing Dallas and wanted to stop him from spending or giving away their money to people like Danny and Travis Walker, the drug dealer who was renting the ranch in Taos. She claimed Dallas was an alcoholic and a drug addict who suffered from dementia and who had to be stopped. That's why she encouraged Travis to facilitate Dallas' drug habit by giving him all the hard drugs he wanted. Then when Dallas overdosed, Belle turned on Travis and ratted him out to the authorities. So she's involved, directly or indirectly, in what happened to all three of them."

Oralia shook her head. "And yet she was kind enough to give me a check for seventy-five thousand dollars."

Fernando smiled. "Well, I offered her a deal she couldn't refuse."

Now Oralia smiled. "I see. So what will happen to Belle?"

Nothing, absolutely nothing," Fernando said. "She covered her tracks well."

Oralia nodded.

"And let's face it, people like Belle have all the money and lawyers they need to get out of almost anything," he said. "Danny and Dallas are dead, and Travis will be in jail for a long time, but she'll return to Austin and continue living the high life she's accustomed to."

Oralia did not respond. Instead she wiped away a single tear that slid down her cheek.

"It's no secret that the criminal justice system delivers justice inequitably," Fernando said. "It suffers from the same inequalities you see in every other aspect of American life."

Oralia sighed. "So I've discovered."

They regarded each other over the desk for a long moment. Then, grimacing, she struggled to stand up while holding her big belly and slowly walked to the door. She opened the door but then stopped and turned around.

"Ruby was right about you," Oralia said.

Fernando laughed. "Good old Ruby, she supports all the losing causes."

Oralia smiled. "Lucky for all of us she does," she said and walked out the door.

READERS GUIDE

1. When local musician Danny Ortiz is murdered in downtown Santa Fe, police assume he was a victim of random violence. His wife Oralia thinks otherwise and asks Private Investigator Fernando Lopez to find her husband's killers. Why does she believe her husband was killed intentionally?

2. Before his murder Danny Ortiz was scheduled to perform with well-known Austin musician Dallas Longstreet, but Longstreet bailed on Danny and checked into a guest ranch in Taos rumored to be a drug ranch operated by a long-time friend of Longstreet's by the name of Travis Walker. Lopez discovers that Danny had gone up to the ranch to persuade Longstreet to leave but was manhandled by two of Walker's bodyguards. Lopez meets much the same fate when goes to the ranch to investigate. What does Lopez find when he arrives at the ranch that strikes him as suspicious? Why is the ranch called Painted Skull Ranch?

3. In Taos Lopez teams up with Taos County Sheriff Hank Mathews. What does Lopez learn about Painted Skull Ranch from Mathews? Why is this information important going forward?

4. Unable to persuade Longstreet to leave the ranch, Lopez visits Longstreet's estranged wife, Belle, currently staying at Bishop's Lodge Resort outside Santa Fe. Describe Belle. How is Lopez received by Belle and her entourage: Paula, Scott, and Larry?

5. Paula comes to see Lopez in his office bringing with her a torn check she'd found in a wastebasket in Larry's room at Bishop's Lodge Resort. The check is made out to Danny and signed by Longstreet himself. What is the significance of this check? What does it suggest to Lopez?

6. Lopez learns from Paula that Belle is currently having an affair and at the same time suing Dallas for divorce. How and where does Lopez discover the identity of Belle's latest fling? What is the significance of this discovery? What does it tell Lopez?

7. Lopez befriends Jerry, the long-time caretaker of Painted Skull Ranch, which is a two-hundred year old ranch owned by Bill Candelaria, the last of the Candelaria family. What important information does Jerry provide Lopez that helps Lopez unravel the secret of Painted Skull Ranch?

8. Painted Skull Ranch has its own Morada, dating from the eighteenth century. What exactly is a Morada? What secret does Lopez discover in the Morada? How does he find the secret?

9. When Dallas dies of a supposed overdose at the ranch, Lopez suspects a conspiracy. Who all is involved in the conspiracy? Who's the leader?

10. After a shoot-out with Walker and his two bodyguards, Walker flees. Lopez and Mathews find him at the St. James Hotel in Cimarron, east of Taos. What is the story behind the St. James Hotel? Why does Mathews warn Lopez?

11. After Walker is apprehended Lopez returns to Santa Fe, where he is ambushed by one of the men working for Belle Longstreet. This event becomes one of the pivotal moments in the story because Lopez realizes who has organized the entire conspiracy, the mastermind. Who is the mastermind?

12. When Lopez finally confronts the mastermind, he knows that 'justice' in the legal sense of the word is not possible, so what punishment or compensation does he exact from the person responsible?

www.ingramcontent.com/pod-product-compliance
Lightning Source LLC
Chambersburg PA
CBHW011349010726
47493CB00011B/3017